THE DESPERATE CYCLE
A NOVEL FROM JAMAICA

TONY TAME

Savant Books and Publications
Honolulu, HI, USA
2013

Published in the USA by Savant Books and Publications
2630 Kapiolani Blvd #1601
Honolulu, HI 96826
http://www.savantbooksandpublications.com

Printed in the USA

Edited by Ashley O'Neil
Cover Photos Courtesy of Brian Rosen
Cover Design by Daniel S. Janik

13-digit ISBN: 978-0-9852506-9-0
10-digit ISNB: 0985250690

DEDICATION

For my son, Sean, and my talented, long-suffering editor, Ashley, who put up with all my lazy ways and did so much to make the book conform to the rules of grammar and punctuation.

The Desperate Cycle

CHAPTER 1

POISON AND POWER IN HIGH PLACES

Mr. Akiyama was an early riser. He had liked the daybreak at home in his orderly nation and he liked it equally well in this less disciplined society in which he now lived. In Japan, if workers were expected to be ready for work at six in the morning, everyone would be ready at that time.

Mr. Akiyama had realized long ago that in Jamaica the arrival time posted on the coffee farm bulletin board and what was set out in the work contracts were simply hopeful and optimistic suggestions. More time would be lost trying to untie skillful excuses concerning family catastrophes, urgent business, travel difficulties and mysterious illnesses than the exercise was worth, so he had adapted to the island style in his own way by being on duty at every daylight hour. This enabled him to deploy his workforce to meet the varied personnel needs.

"Where is Natty and his brother today?"

"Dem gone to Portland to buy a donkey. Dem granny tell me fe tell you, suh."

"Then you go with Stumble Man. Work with him today."

"I don't know dat work so good, Mr. Akky. I never do the spray work before."

"You will by the time they get back with their donkey!"

The result was that, gradually, every employee had developed skill in all aspects of endeavor on the coffee farm. Mr. Akiyama's directors were so pleased that they had left him in charge long after a normal rotation ought to have seen him promoted to a senior position in the home office. This was also pleasing to Mr. Akiyama who had already fathered two children in adjacent mountain villages and was presently waiting to see if a third would be confirmed by experts in rural DNA techniques, namely skin, hair and eye coloring.

This morning was enshrouded in mist and sharply cold as most mornings were in the high country, where they grow Blue Mountain Coffee to perfection. From the manager's office, Mr. Akiyama dispatched the men to their tasks on various sections of the estate. The mountain smells peculiar to the cultivation of this extremely valuable crop, which does best in altitudes between two and four thousand feet, wafted through the open windows of his office.

When the daily routine began to wane after a few hours (it would have been a twenty-minute matter if the full complement of staff had all been ready and waiting to start at the prescribed time), Mr. Akiyama sent for his chief supervisor.

This year the pest known as the coffee borer had become more widespread than usual and everyone agreed that something had to be done about the infestation. There were some fainthearted fellows down at the university who brought up what they considered "areas of grave environmental concern" about the effects of constant chemical intervention.

Fortunately, they generally got the sort of attention given to people who spend their days talking to themselves or trying to convince the public that they are reincarnations of Napoleon. Up here, where serious men are dealing with an agricultural commodity that ranks with marijuana as a foreign exchange earner, all that fretfulness about hillside waterways becoming "arteries of poison," was just so much static. Imagine using a phrase like that!

Nonetheless, that was exactly how a young scientist, aided and abetted by a beady-eyed lady from some green group, had described a few of the rivers. All they need to do to gain proper perspective is come and look at these streams and they would be able to see for themselves that there is plenty of good old normal water still in them, even if they do look a little cloudy sometimes. And so what if the river crayfish and mountain minnows seem to have almost disappeared? Every now and then you still see one. That's the way it goes.

If you work on a proper coffee farm, you can earn good money and go out and buy yourself a pound of imported shrimp or a tin of Canadian sardines. Who wants to spend a day trying to snare a river janga, as the crayfish are called, by lying on your stomach on the bank of a stream among grass lice or trying to catch a half pound of little darters with a piece of mosquito netting?

Maybe the kids got a bit of fun out of it, but now they can stay indoors and watch television. Yes, you can buy one of those too with the coffee wages.

The field supervisor came in and sat facing Mr. Akiyama's desk. Through the wide windows, the panoramic beauty of what is known as the Grand Ridge of the Blue Mountains was undergoing that transition stage of the morning when the constantly changing angle of the rising sun was chasing one color after another as light probed between the peaks and flanks of the lush valleys.

If the Western Taíno tribes, who inhabited these regions before destiny and disease exterminated them, had climbed to such heights in this land of wood and water, it must have looked to them as unspoiled as it did today from the north window of the manager's office. Mr. Akiyama and his operations supervisor—who had been a small-scale coffee planter himself until the conglomerate from Japan bought his land and gave him a job—both appreciated this wonderful view. They were men who knew a good thing when they saw it.

"This is a very good thing," Mr. Akiyama said. He put the product sample in its neat plastic container with all the required cautions listed on the packaging on his desk.

The supervisor examined it. The bottle looked small in his large farmer's hands. "Is that a new label on it?" he asked.

"Oh, yes. They are always coming up with new labels."

"But works the same?"

"It *is* the same, only 'the names have been changed to protect the innocent'."

"Me knew it as Thiodan," the supervisor said.

"Well, meet Tiovel."

"Me hope it strong like the old one. The borers are all over the place."

"It is as strong as you make it. Here are the directions which are the same as before. They are guidelines, of course. Use your experience about dilution."

That year there were exceptionally heavy rains and the wet season lasted uncharacteristically long. Rivers, swollen overnight to torrents, broke records as they tore little mountain bridges away from the dissolving banks separating villages from one another. Roadsides collapsed and fell away. Just when any reasonable man would have assumed the deluge was going to abate and let business get going again, back came the huge clouds, swelling dark and massive over the highest peaks which towered above the most elevated cultivations, ready to unload more water from the sky all over man's industry and valiant effort.

Fortunately, intelligent management took proper care to have emergency preparations for such aberrant behavior by uncooperative, irresponsible nature. Competent administrators made sure that there were stocks of whatever material might be wasted by being washed down the slopes into the lowlands via turbulent short-lived streams feeding the bigger rivers.

In coffee farming, the bottom line is clearly demarcated in dollars and that is drawn and calculated and directs those activities which take place in the exquisite country where clouds and forests and men dwell together. It is certainly not done down in valleys where the raging run-offs feed into the cresting rivers rushing on their journey to the sea, doing their job of flushing and cleaning the land, carrying all before them as they race toward the great mother of life from whence came the creatures of the land.

CHAPTER 2

TIDYING UP

The new Member of Parliament parked his silver-gray four-wheel drive sport utility vehicle on the embankment which inclined upward as it led to the cement cap topping the cut-stone wall of the town gully. His now-retired predecessor had paved the old bed of the ravine and then walled the sides at only about four times what the whole project ought to have cost. This old fellow had three brothers in the construction business and one could not expect to maintain family status and completely avoid a little favoritism. Even the political party which had recently catapulted him into his present position had a slogan that said: *Share the Wealth*.

Two bored-looking representatives from the Public

Works Division walked with the Member of Parliament to the edge of the twenty-foot wide culvert. The smell was bad enough back where they had left the vehicles. Up here, it was unbelievable.

All along the bank, in both directions, small and not-so-small pipes stuck out over the edge of the parapet and, occasionally, fluids of various viscosities poured out of the mouths of these conduits. There was a steady stream of milky liquid coursing between the accumulations of garbage and discarded appliances, tins, and less identifiable objects which littered the floor of the drain. Sheets of cardboard, strands of fiberglass matting, cloth and plastic bags clung temporarily to these obstacles and to places where the cement paving had broken and left up-thrust jagged ridges. These splintered surfaces are a trade mark of the rapid deterioration of structures built by blending a tiny amount of cement, a generous helping of unwashed sand, some muddy stones and a huge infusion of grassroots politics.

The three men looked at the scene for as long as they could stand it and then hurried back to their cars. Down there it was bearable with the mid-morning wind now beginning to come in from the nearby open bay. This wide, crescent beach was the seafront for the town. The salt smell on the breeze functioned as an atmospheric disinfectant.

"Do you think you can do anything about it?" the Member of Parliament asked, because that is what he had to ask.

"We can look into it, but the budget can't stand a big fix-up, as you are well aware. Perhaps we can get a tractor from the sugar estate to help. I mean, to help by pushing the heavy stuff out into the sea. It would look a lot better right away and some of the other stuff would flow out quick and then float off. For a while, anyhow."

"Well, try that. That sounds like an excellent plan. We have to do something. The people are onto me all the time. Why you think I hardly ever go to the constituency office? I'm not the minister of finance. I can't print money like him. What you want me to tell them?"

"Tell them to stop throwing everything into it. That's why it is like that."

"They say the people further up do it. And the factory that makes and bottles the bleach. That's what they say."

"The people further up have all those pipes you just

saw? The ones all along the edges right here in town?"

"If I start on that they are going to ask about a new sewage system, and where is the money going to come for that if you don't even have the cash to repave the floor of the drain? You want me to start blaming the factory when it is practically the only employer around this place? I'm not getting into that argument. Me look like a madman to you?" Emotion was forcing him into the vernacular. He took a deep breath to reassert his position and command of the language. "Listen seriously now. You think you can really get a tractor? How soon?"

"I'll go and see about it this afternoon."

The man who had originally brought up the tractor idea said, "It's a good thing the harbor is fairly deep just in front here. If you just push it to where the edge is, then the whole mess goes right down and you never see any of the big stuff again. It's soft mud beyond there. We've done it before, lots of times, and they have a driver up at the sugar estate that knows just how far out he can go before he and the machine all go down into the mud. The other drivers won't do it because they think it's dangerous.

"Those younger ones don't know where the hard

parts of the ground are. They just shove it a little way out and bits of the junk show up at low tide and even wash back up, especially if you get a big wind before it can get sunk down and anchored properly. But that old fellow knows that there is no danger at all if you go right to near the deep part. He knows the firm places. He'll get rid of it nicely for us. It's not dangerous at all if we get him. We've done it lots of times. We can get it on the cheap if you okay the job on a basis of no receipt required."

"Get him, get him," the Member of Parliament said. He sounded slightly hysterical. "Don't bother me with details. I have to go now. I am late at visiting the office. I leave all this with you."

The Member of Parliament drove cautiously past his office. He noticed with relief that nobody appeared to be standing around outside the front. Nonetheless, he was still uncertain. You could never trust these people. They were some damn tricky ones. And mean spirited. Sometimes disaffected voters were watching from some hiding place across the street as predators do when employing natural cover during the stalking of their prey. He thought of these critics in much the same way Russian —and, later, American—troops had regarded the

Mujahidin snipers in Afghanistan: a constant, deadly peril. Although he was comparatively young at the job, he had already begun to develop the skills of the hunted animal, so essential in the practice of his present trade.

He drove up the side street and walked through an alley to the back entrance. He was developing a tic below his right eye. A newspaper critic of his administration had commented on it, saying that it gave him a "furtive" look.

For a moment, it occurred to him that this was a hell of a way to make a living, this dodging around like some wrongdoer, but he was acutely aware of the attendant benefits and potential future of being an elected official. He was equally sensitive to the fact that the greatest contrast in the whole world of employment was between being an elected official, with at least some connection to power, and an unelected ex-official with zero connections and not even an association with power. The very thought made him shudder.

He could hear the old caretaker, who he had inherited along with the slightly dilapidated office, coughing inside. The Member of Parliament decided he would have to get somebody healthier and less ghostly eventually, but not now. This tubercular specter was very cheap. The Member of Parliament called to him softly. The man opened the door. He had a big smile on his stubbly, wrinkled face. Inside, the Member of Parliament saw that a window facing the side street was broken and there was a black plastic bag tied to a stone on the floor beneath.

"Lucky the broken glass never cut it open," the old fellow said cheerfully. "It's a bag of shit."

"Oh, God! Listen, Benny, I have to go into Kingston for a meeting immediately, but tell anyone who comes around that I have personally made arrangements with specially trained heavy equipment operators outfitted with the appropriate machinery to start work on the drain. This is being done as we speak. The project will be under qualified supervisors organized and handpicked by me from the scientific division of the ministry. I have arranged all this. I am a problem solver. Make sure you tell it to them just like that. Bottom line is this: I have it under control and they will see that I can take care of it. Spread the word. Try and remember all that. And clean up this place. Please do that. Do it now. And put some paper or a piece of wood or something over the broken pane." He was a problem solver, all right.

After the Member of Parliament had left, taking his usual precautions, the ancient janitor slipped the offending bag onto a sheet of newspaper with the aid of a piece of cardboard. He considered for a moment putting it into the municipal garbage container in front of the office, but knew how irregularly this was emptied and was sure that in an hour or two other sharp pointed items thrown into it would open this little message to his boss thereby inviting all sorts of low humor. Then there was his personal comfort to be considered as well. His salary was so miniscule he had been evicted from the crumbling house where he had rented a room and was now living in the office on an unofficial basis. Why should he suffer the inhalation of communications between the constituents and their political representative?

The caretaker had been around a long time and was a problem solver in his own right.

He folded the newspaper up into a parcel and set off toward the gully. The gully was clearly the right place for it.

The gully which led to the sea.

CHAPTER 3

FACING FACTS

At the treatment plant they had opened the last of the bypass routes that fed untreated effluent directly past the increasingly rusting and cracked array of settlement beds and holding tanks. Emergency measures like this were incorporated into the original design as is normal with such facilities.

You could use this procedure if a storm damaged the pumps or blocked the inlet grates. It was there as a fallback position should an earthquake or some other unforeseen event of major dimension occur, rupturing a tank. If that happened, you could discharge a portion, or, in a real catastrophe, the entire flow, straight into the sea while you tackled the crisis.

And the sea took it. That's what it does. Most of

mankind has always reasonably assumed that is what the sea is there for. It looks big enough to take care of us and itself as well. And it has been there for an awfully long time. It is patient and forgiving to insults. Presumably, it will take corrective measures, but, perhaps with a little luck, not in our lifetime. That's the generally held, convenient truth.

This particular crisis that led to the final surrender by the personnel at the plant was not confined to a single tank or an individual pump. This was a crisis that affected the entire operation. It was called a crisis, but the term was really used quite incorrectly in this case since the word carries a sense of temporariness. It had begun with a single pump failure and so the "crisis" phrase terminology came into employment with some legitimacy. When no finances were identified to cope with that incident, the crisis had begun to spread to other overworked equipment and finally to the funds being "unavailable" for all the treatment chemicals. At that point, they opened the seaward sluice gates which short-circuited the plant and everyone waited for the extended crisis to be resolved.

That was thirty years ago.

They still have a staff on location to keep the flow-through operational, although there is not much for them to do. There is a man there now, nearing retirement, who was a young trainee manager when the system was still working normally. He had been part of a hopeful band that believed and trusted in what was known and categorized in the nineteen-seventies as the then Prime Minister Michael Manley's philosophy of *Better Must Come*. This was to be achieved by a combination of Democratic Socialism and wishful thinking presented in a cocktail of revolutionary fervor and patriotic rhetoric. The manner of paying for the "better" had never been specified or even tentatively identified. When he had opened the last barrier, this man had felt as though he had literally punched his own country in the guts.

From his little cubicle in the deteriorating building on the compound, this veteran, who was now classified as the overseer—the term manager would have carried a higher salary—could see the gradual effects of the high nutrient levels in the harbor as the decades passed. The first sign had been the red tides.

Once only brief occurrences, there now came regular, prolonged "blooms" of red tide. This is the popular name for the wine-colored water that results from algal imbalance in the water column. Fish, with their central nervous system destroyed, would actually come to the toxic water's edge and die there, seeking relief in a few last gulps of pure oxygen from the now-poisoned element of their creation. With the passage of time, this phenomenon began to disappear because water can get to a point where even specific algae have a problem surviving in it. At that stage, the water finally goes from red to dead. Or nearly dead. For the sea never truly gives up.

The pelicans that had once perched in numbers along the fences of the treatment plant had been reduced to a few scruffy survivors. Some had clearly observable swellings on their bodies. The overseer had not seen a young pelican in the last five years.

"We have killed our beautiful harbor. I am an accomplice to murder," he had written to his director on a famous occasion. He had been a well-educated young man which was why he had been selected as a trainee manager in the first place. The director had summoned him to his immaculate office in the air-conditioned building, where such exalted persons roosted, and handed him back the letter containing the shocking message with its reference to marine homicide. "Please, Mr. Barton," the director, who was really a kind-natured man, had said, "do not ruin your future with the assumption of dramatic positions. There is no future in it. No future at all."

The director had invited him to tear up the offending missive in front of him. And he had done so. It had not been very much harder than opening the valves had been. Everybody has to try to keep on making a living and he was no exception. That was the bottom line. The good old bottom line phrase again. That's the problem we all have to solve somehow.

When he contemplated his pension, which would only be a fraction of his present paltry wages, he felt real panic. He knew that sometimes faithful workers of many years' service could be retained as watchmen at their old workplaces to supplement the pittance which government pensioners got until they did everybody a favor and died, thus taking a tiny fractional strain off the state's expenses.

He considered the prospect of having a word about this possibility of extended employment to the current director. If he could get that watchman's post, plus the pension, he figured that, knowing the facility so well, he could actually live here and hold on to existence like the last of the distressed pelicans. Almost the whole of the office space was vacant anyhow. Nobody would care about that technical breach of regulations. There were caretakers living at their places of employment all over the country.

Thinking about such prospects, he went on looking wistfully out the window of his present office and, maybe, future home. He was watching the steady stream of untreated, fetid fluid pouring down the spillway into the harbor. Just a mile away, the still blue ship channel opening to the ocean was clearly visible, and that was where it was going.

CHAPTER 4

THE SOCIAL AND ECONOMIC SCENE

The pecking order in the artisan fishing industry of Jamaica is not extremely strict. Still, there are some general distinctions. Men who captain bigger boats and operate more powerful engines are going to be better regarded in the community and are likely to have more money and prettier women at home than some patient, starving unfortunate who hangs around until the herring-net guys finish shaking and picking the still-quivering silver prizes from the mesh, then pack the fish and the webbing inside the boat and head off to where the vendors are waiting for the catch.

At that point, the waiting human scavenger moves in on the spot where the netters were working and combs the sea floor for leftovers which have fallen unnoticed and, in any case, not worth the trouble of locating on a one-by-one basis. Under no circumstances are these two levels of maritime harvesting going to be regarded as quite equal.

Like other business structures, there is also migration up and down the scale. A few, very few, progress steadily upward. Some move entirely out of the cycle of punishing hours and battering life in the trenches carved between the endless swells to become land-based boat owners and distributors of the product. Some—once again, an infinitesimal number—even obtain vans and join in the more capital intensive distribution branch of the operation. As a general rule, the only ones who succeed truly at this level are those who have come through the mill of the actual fishing itself where the rollers of the ocean grind, and grind exceeding small. That is because these veterans know how the whole business really works.

Many are the investors who have noticed that there is a huge differential between what a man earns when he arrives in the daybreak, soaked and sleepless, from a night trying to convince yellowtail snappers that a dead minnow pinned on a hook is worth betting its life against, and the final retail price. This type of mid-night fishing reduces men to a permanently red-eyed, shaky state induced by working in the darkness with the shaded, hissing, clear-glass pressure lamp as the one source of light in that otherwise pitching black world. They typically drink a flask of straight white rum to bring back their energy level before facing any morning breakfast, that is, if you can call it breakfast after you have already been up for fourteen hours. For many rum *is* their breakfast, another reason why they are shaky and look as they do.

The long cold nights, alcohol and other drugs may dull the senses a bit, but these night fishermen are not fools. After all, they make their living outwitting fish and many say that fish are brain food. So if the shore-bound, remote control owner is an untutored entrant into the fishing industry, who has started on the basis that he will purchase a motorboat and make a good living, plus pay for the equipment, but is unaware of exactly what the outcome might prove to be, he is at a huge disadvantage.

There are a hundred reasons why a particular night may produce a poor catch. The current was too strong. The fish must have moved up, down, in, further out. The water was too cold, too hot. Sharks were everywhere and made the snapper wild. They were just not biting—must be waiting on the change of moon. They will probably show up tomorrow night. For any of those and other reasons that can be invented, the catch is all too often pitiful. But sometimes it is not.

This is when the battered crew who has suffered through gloomy nights of heaving swells and flying spray begin considering the inexperience of a novice entrepreneur. A graduate of the university of war against boiling seas and tireless hunting during the eternal darkness is not going to be tricked easily because he is constantly functioning as a spymaster, obtaining insider information all along the coast and from a network of friends who are still fighting on the front line. He will put up with the bad production only when it falls in line with his own experience and the feedback gleaned from men he trusts.

This is not the case with the intrepid beginner. He joined the game too far up in the hierarchy to have these hard-earned advantages. This inexperience is a fatal flaw in his business plan. So, now, the crew stop briefly on the way in to their homeport and sell all the highest quality fish from one of these "good" nights to other buyers and sell them quickly too because they can give an excellent discount. They don't have to worry about paying the installments on the boat.

"If the engine breaks down that's not our fault, boss. We did tell you to get a better one. We did tell you that if you get a really powerful one it lasts longer. Remember that, boss? You have to spend money to make money, right?"

That's the kind of problem facing the dry, clean and rested fellow waiting expectantly for them at the place where the boat is moored. And he is going to hear that the fish must have moved up, down, in, further out, or, if they can think of it, some brand new convincing explanation that will keep him quiet until the much awaited day when he walks away from the whole thing in disgust and goes into hiding from his creditors and the remains of the whole shattered enterprise gets picked up for a song. Plenty of men get boats this way and obtain higher social status, and more comely ladies, as a consequence.

So there are all sorts of reasons why the beach will accommodate people at various levels of the ladder of success, but there exists a quiet respect for even the least prominent members of the community because everybody in the fraternity knows how hard it really is and a man who keeps at it is still a man. He gets as wet and chilled and faces the uncertainties of the weather and the trade as does everyone else.

Like all of us, even the boy or old man collecting the bycatch that drifts to the sea floor when the nets are sifted is just trying to hold on as best as he can. And massive equalizers such as hurricanes, and other forces not well understood as yet, lurk in the uncertain future so it is wise to retain the brotherhood. Therefore, let us not practice casual disdain. The grip on a livelihood obtained from the sea is always tenuous. As Avril Lavigne reminds us in the ballad of the same name, the trick is to keep holding on.

A man named Pedro was doing just that. He was holding on to the life his father had bequeathed to him and it showed. Night fishing had aged him prematurely as it does all who follow that profession. It just seemed to do it faster with him.

One day he sat down in the damp sand beside his small boat feeling suddenly dizzy. He woke up later in the hospital where a fish vendor with an open-backed truck had taken him.

The vendor was a sympathetic but practical man and had offered to take the unconscious Pedro to the town hospital because it was on his way. Two fishermen put a flattened out cardboard box over the vendor's load of fish and placed Pedro on top of it. Given time, they would have removed the box staples, but they figured it was urgent and Pedro didn't look like he would feel a few little old staple ends in his present state. The vendor had said, "Spread him out as much as you can. Don't let him curl up and put too much weight in one spot and squash the snapper. Them yellowtail can't take any pressure. You know them is a soft type of fish."

When they arrived at the public hospital the receiving staff had complained that Pedro smelled funny. They discussed who should carry him inside. He had rolled partially off the cardboard and a lot of him was mixed up in the catch. The vendor asked them if they were going to take him out or did they expect him to carry Pedro around to all the hotels where he was going to sell the fish. How would that look? How would that sound when hc told all those big hotel purchasing managers that the hospital left Pedro in there rolling around with the snappers?

"You think that will be good for you or me? Stop shake your head like idiot! Get the old man out and fix him up or throw him away or whatever you do here and let me try to go on with making a living. Times is hard. You all get paid no matter if people in this broken down joint you pretend is a hospital live or die, but not me! Me don't have it so rass good. If you don't take him out, mek me tell you shits what me is going to do. Me going to tie a rope to his foot and tie the other end to your door and drive off. What you going to do then? You bunch of civil servants going to stop me? Take him backside out and then go wash your hands. You don't have soap in this place?"

Once they got Pedro inside, one of the porters, still brushing scales from his uniform, noticed that the patient's eyes were half open.

"Wake up, old man," they advised him. "Try and wake up so we can put you in a chair. We don't want to put you on the floor. That floor is not so clean. We don't get no disinfectant for about a week. Money shortage, you know."

You see? They were not heartless men, just ordinary

people who grow defensive calluses on their sensibilities in order to cope with life as they found it. Everybody adjusts to their job.

They were trying to balance Pedro on a chair when a young doctor came out of the casualty room and, looking at the scene in the waiting room, said, "Bring the old fellow in here."

"Look at how you is lucky," one of the porters said. "You get treatment right as you come. They must think you is a VIP. Don't count on that next time, old man. The doctor never smelled you yet." The other porter who had helped carry Pedro inside laughed. Everyone needs some humor to get through the long days.

When the young doctor took Pedro's blood pressure he read it and waited a little while and then did it again before he wrote the figures down. "Can you hear me?" he asked.

Pedro tried to say something, but it came out wrong so he just nodded. For the rest of his short life after that he sometimes spoke a little oddly.

They kept him at the hospital for a few days and tried to explain to him that he must have had very high, untreated blood pressure for a long time, probably since his youth, and had developed an enlarged heart. The doctor told him things about kidneys and some part of him they called arteries. All of it was incomprehensible to him. He was going to have to take some pills every day and try and take it easy. The hospital only had one of the three varieties of pills that were prescribed because they ran out all the time, but the town pharmacy had all of them.

If he could have obtained the drugs from the hospital they would have been free of charge, but the pharmacy was another matter. After a patient reached a certain age there was a special drug program called *Drugs for the Elderly*, but Pedro, although he was commonly called "old man," was only forty-five. Consequently, he adjusted his medication on purely financial grounds.

He decided to take it easy for a week. A friend brought around some food and said, "Take it easy. Cool out, old man." This friend had secured all of Pedro's tackle when he had passed out on the beach and brought it up to his house. No one would have stolen it, but delivering it was a gesture of fellowship and equality in the face of circumstance. Who might be next?

Pedro used the enforced vacation to fix up all of his lines and cut off the suspect hooks that needed replacing and put a new brace on the wooden lamp stand. One of his arms still functioned poorly since that day he passed out on the beach, but he could use it. His only son, whose name was Fitzroy, called Sprinter in honor of his reputation as a promising athlete in track and field events, was going to have to take over the responsibility of getting the bait. That was clear now with Pedro's arm problem. Sprinter had been doing that job occasionally, but he would have to take it more seriously now. Since he was still technically in high school (though with less and less regularity than met with the institution's approval), it looked like even his sporadic attendance was now in question.

The old cycle of poverty, general neglect and lack of education was beginning to gather him, as it had gathered so many, into its orbit.

Pedro's fishing system was at the low end of the spectrum of recognized methods. His boat was small and the engine a wheezing ghost of its former self. At one time, Pedro had set quite a few wire traps. These have a limited lifespan and the cost of the galvanized wire mesh had gone up disproportionately to the returns which traps set within the practical range his doubtful vessel could cover. So he had descended slightly in the hierarchy of the trade.

He became a "*palanca*" fisherman.

No one seems to know where this name comes from, but it is recognized island wide. There is nothing unique in it. Variations are in use all over the world, with million dollar "long lines" being at the ultimate peak of the profession and Pedro's version occupying the lowest bracket. This "poor man's long line" is simply a few hundred yards of sixty-pound breaking strain monofilament line with a heavy sinker at each end and small hooks connected by a much lighter line placed at regular intervals of about six feet.

The idea behind the design of using the weaker line on the short connection between the "mother line" and the baited hook is built around the hope that if something really awful, like a shark or a big ray, should ingest either the bait or a small fish that is already hooked, this trace or leader, as the weaker line is sometimes called, should break, thus saving the rest of the assembly from destruction.

Naturally, design flaws show up in inventions all the way from the space shuttle to the *palanca* line. In the latter, it is somewhat easier to understand these shortcomings by those lacking degrees in engineering.

Let us examine this weakness.

A large predator may not confine himself to one fish or one bait and may prowl the line, feeding as he goes, and can get wound up in the main strand. If the big fish rolls or twists a few times he can get a dozen or more of the small hooks buried in various parts of his anatomy. At that point, the combined strength of the quantity of numerous pieces of fine linking line is equal to or greater than that of the central connector.

If that happens, the best outcome that can be reasonably expected is that the annoyed monster manages to bite through the mother line, leaving the owner with a remnant section upon which to attempt a resurrection. If that does not happen, then the shark, or whatever it happens to be, will set course out into the open ocean, trailing the entire investment with him, or scraping it off on the outer reefs if he can, or carrying it around for a while like an annoying cloud of nylon threading. In that case, the encumbrance will keep this already crotchety animal in a really bad mood.

That is one of the drawbacks inherent in this type of mechanism. When it takes place, you lose all, or part, of the line. Bad, but not fatal in the classic sense. But suppose it happens while you are taking the line in. These unsophisticated versions of the big budget long line do not have individual detachable hooks. These hooks are permanently tied to the mother line.

Imagine what is likely to transpire if you have a few hundred hooks aboard when something occurs like the sudden appropriation by an unwelcome visitor of the unrecovered section of the *palanca* which is still in the water. What is going to happen is all those hooks are going to start whizzing overboard as the line peels out.

If that should happen, you have at most a minute or two to lock the line around something firm, like a cleat, so that the unknown enemy force deployed against you can cut or break it. If you don't secure it quickly enough then you are going to have all those hooks coming from behind, zooming out past you and heading wherever the new infuriated owner of the *palanca* is going. If a few of these find solid, random lodging in your person then you could discover yourself in an identical situation to that of the living submarine on the other end. You are back up against the scientific fact that enough of these attachments equals or exceeds the breaking point of the mother line so the only thing to do is hope the hooks, interrupted in their flight by your body, tear out. This is a reasonable, though painful, expectation since most of a human is quite fleshy, the skin weak, and the hooks sharp. So all may not be lost.

Even an eye is a fair exchange for freedom from such an unplanned entanglement. An ear lobe is a minor inconvenience. If luck really deserts you, then contemplate becoming a lifelong companion of the creature now in control at the other end, yoked together in a terrifying voyage through the underwater world. It will only be terrifying for as long as the remainder of your then limited life expectancy might be. After a little while, it won't make any difference to you. A few practitioners of this art have gone this way, leaving only a craft bereft of man and line to attest to the manner of their sudden departure.

All these considerations help keep the *palanca* fisherman properly awake and dutifully alert during the long nights spent tending the line which is marked at each end with a little platform fitted with a flaming "bottle lamp" tied on top of it, which is a glass bottle filled with kerosene and a cloth wick pushed in through the mouth. *Palanca* fishing is a low-rent occupation so all the equipment is constrained by basic economics. Bottom line accounting—there's that phrase again—at its most primitive. Those who follow this branch of the fishing trade must adjust everything—medication, equipment and so on—within a very tight budget.

Pedro had a talk with his son Sprinter.

He explained that the new burden of becoming bait provider full time was now going to become his responsibility. There are a variety of options here. The finest involves buying imported, frozen, packaged squid at a supermarket. That is usually beyond Pedro's pay grade.

"So we are stuck with what we can catch ourselves, boy."

It is necessary that Sprinter understand all the technicalities now that he is going to have to participate on a daily basis in the tricky, uncertain business of earning a living: the adult conundrum.

On some parts of the island there are a lot of

diminutive mollusk-type animals called "red conch." Each one makes excellent bait because it is tough and durable and not subject to easy disintegration. The difficulty is they are only found with any regularity in certain places and very seasonal where Pedro lives, so he had always depended on shove netting and cast netting. Sprinter should now grasp that, since his father's left arm is unreliable and likely to stay that way for the foreseeable future, both of these endeavors were not really practical for Pedro to handle any longer.

"It's your turn, my boy."

In shove netting, you walk in shallow water and shove a roughly triangular frame with a net stretched loosely over the sea floor. Hence the name. The widest part of the triangle is forced along the seabed and small shrimps, in response to the disturbance, jump up from the grass and mud and get scooped into the balloon formed by the net following the wooden structure. You need two good arms for that work. The cast net equally requires unimpaired arms to gather, hold and spread it out in one powerful heave over the schools of suitable bait fish.

Sprinter, who had arms as strong and capable as his legs, was to assume the job of selecting which of these implements would be most appropriate on each day and ensure that there was enough bait to keep Pedro supplied for the night. Failure at this spelled failure to eat, so it was not something to be taken lightly.

Sprinter had been a second rate student, and had never been able to develop a great interest in the atmosphere of the classroom, so the prospect of curtailed school attendance did not distress him greatly. Nonetheless, he was to continue with as much classroom time as could be accommodated within the limits of these new grave responsibilities. It was as simple as that.

Sprinter was well placed to understand the situation because his best friend Rocky, a tough little orphan well known around the beach as a good diver, had faced much the same circumstances of having to grow up quickly when his father had been accidently shot in an alleged shootout between a police patrol and some mysterious criminals who disappeared without a trace. A report to the effect that these vanished miscreants had drawn guns and fired upon the forces of law and order had been circulated showing that the police had been faced with no option other than to return fire. Very unfortunate, but it happens with such regularity!

It must certainly have been a genuine accident because Rocky's father never had the reputation of being any kind of troublemaker. His only known failing was a tendency to stay extremely late at the bar and leave in a stumbling condition. Going home like that, he often bumped into people on the dark streets of the waterfront. Everyone knew he couldn't help it and they took it good naturedly. Surely, nobody could get shot for accidentally bumping into people? That would be out of the question in a civilized country. Anyone guilty of perpetrating such an act would be a murderer.

The Desperate Cycle

CHAPTER 5

A BAD NIGHT

Sprinter had waded almost two miles, going as carefully and quietly as he could, and was at the end of the curving stretch of green mangrove forest. Beyond that, the stone-strewn shore began which provided no shelter for the small schools of juvenile herring and the fry that mixed with them. A few times he had cast the net blindly under the overhanging leaves in tiny coves that were usually reliable, but only got a few of what they called "tough heads." These were ugly, blunt-shaped, small fish which nothing would eat under any conditions. They must die of old age.

This was the second day running that he had failed at providing bait and he was going to try the shove net in the muddy place. If there were any shrimps to be found that is where they would be. It was the only thing left. But he was lacking in confidence which was not his normal frame of mind. He had been worried ever since he had seen the dead eels along the edge of the breakwater this morning. Eels were notoriously rugged survivalist types and they could handle most natural challenges. Yet there were dozens of dead bloated ones on the mud bank and floating in front of it. He had never seen that before.

And the water smelled different since the big rains. He wasn't sure what made it smell that way. It smelled of death.

Pedro saw Sprinter coming back to the fishing beach and did not have to ask how the bait catching had gone. The father knew from the slope of his son's shoulders and the dragging pace how bad things were.

Before Sprinter could say anything, his father said, "It's all right. Me don't know what's wrong with the water either. But me did talk to Mr. Chin at the store and he gave me this box of squid on credit. Him is all right, that Chinaman. Go up by the marina tonight with the net when me go out and see if anything come around the bright lights on the wharf. It might be enough for tomorrow. If me cut the squid small some might be left. Me can mix it with the fresh stuff if you get anything later. See if you have any luck there. That watchman is an okay man. Him pretend all de time that we never go there or covers up for us in some way. Come and help me when me get in. This arm is bad today."

"Very bad?"

"No, just feels weak. It not very bad."

That night, the old engine quit before Pedro got to where he planned to set the line. There was a smell of steam coming from it. He pulled on the starter cord a few times, but the jerking motion traveled all across his chest and he was afraid that it would do more damage to the traitor arm with which he was already annoyed because of its failure to do a fair share of the work.

Where he had reached, by the time the old engine faltered and stopped, was a place that sometimes held a few red snapper and black grunt so he decided to start. He set about lighting the lamp. It was not as far as he had intended to go, but there was an old beach saying about going "past fish to look for fish" so he would retest that proverb tonight. The night wind was steady off the shore and the boat would drift as he let the line out, stretching the line as he went. If the worse came to the worst, and the engine did not start later, he could row home. Even the shirker arm could do that. The engine usually did start after a while anyway. Maybe it needed lots of rest. Pedro had a degree of understanding for it and the weaknesses within it. But he could not help a vague feeling of annoyance and distrust with it—like his arm.

He submerged his right hand in the water and it felt cooler than usual. That was the rain water mixed in with the salt. There had to be plenty of fresh water to affect it all the way to the top. Generally, it sank below the lighter, warmer saline water.

He could see the distant lightning over the high black bulk of the mountains and the clouds which looked like ragged skullcaps. *It must be still raining up there*, he thought. The wind was cold as it came off the drenched land.

Back on the beach, Sprinter had begun his nocturnal search for bait. He was at the perimeter of the town marina where the chain link metal mesh fence went out a few feet into the water which was actually a slightly illegal encroachment. There was some old law that said you could not "obstruct access to land between the high and low tide levels," but it hardly applied to people like owners of marinas and hotels. Possibly, it came down to enforcement or, more likely, how orders were given to the enforcers.

Sprinter could have gone around the barrier, which only went out into the sea to where the depth was about three feet, but there was a loose flap of mesh just where the dry land met the water. Everybody knew where the flap was. He unhooked the two wire strands which considerate intruders always kept in place to facilitate locking and unlocking this unofficial door. Once on the premises of the marina, he walked down to the long concrete T-shaped dock where the ten big arc lights were spaced equally along the seaward front. They cast wide pools of yellow light beneath them. He examined each bright patch carefully. It was just after ten p.m. and he had given the lights enough time to collect whatever was likely to be attracted to the circles of illumination.

As soon as he started, he noticed how quiet it was. If the bait had been around, there should have been small flicking sounds as they circled and made little dashes at the miniature creatures on which they fed. Nonetheless, he made a complete search before he sat down at the end of the pier and accepted the fact that the water was devoid of life.

He saw the watchman coming along. That was all right. There would be no problem there.

"Hello, Watchie," said Sprinter, putting the cast net down on the concrete deck with an air of finality. "You think they will come out later?"

"Me don't see any all this week. Them is getting scarce. You went up along the mangrove?"

"All day. Watchie, you see any dead fish around here?"

"One or two. Not many. But the water smells bad. It's not bad so you can notice most days when the wind comes up, but if it get calm you can smell it in the day. At night when the wind comes round and gets blocked by the building is when you notice it more. Don't you smell it?"

"Me smell it. Out on the mud flats and by the mangroves it stinks worse."

"This harbor is wide open. That's why you don't see much dead fish. Just the ones that have a nature that stops them traveling. The rest of them check out. Everybody have to find a way out and them is no different."

A man opened a sliding glass door on an old, but well kept yacht tied up in a slip near where Sprinter and the watchman were talking. The man climbed up stiffly from the stern of the boat onto the dock. He was a man in late middle age with a big belly. He did not look anywhere near as well maintained as his boat. He had a glass in his hand.

"Hi, Mr. Miller," he said to the watchman. "Did anyone come to the gate with anything for me?"

"No, Captain. Me would know. They would push the bell."

"Who's this?" asked the man who sounded like an American, but one who had been all over the place. He drained the glass in one long swallow.

"We call him Sprinter. His father is a fisherman. Me asked him to buy a dinner for me and he just brought it up by the office. He's a good boy. Don't give no trouble. Everybody know him and his father. Him is just going."

"Well," said the captain, "I'll see you again. Take care, boy." The captain took a look at his glass and seemed shocked to discover that it was empty. He hurried back aboard his boat.

There was nothing further to be done to advance the bait situation.

Sprinter left the marina through the same breach in the fence that he had entered and went back down to the beach where his father would come in. It might not be until daybreak depending on how the night went, but he was worried about the water and the smell and thought he would wait in case the old man quit after just one set.

He made himself as comfortable as possible, sitting against the gear shed with the dry, unused upper part of the cast net as a cushion for his head. A boat came in quietly further down the shoreline. He knew the crew, as he knew all the people of the beach, but he stayed quietly where he was out of tiredness and a sudden desire to retreat into silence. They would not see him in the shadow of the hut and perhaps he could sleep for a bit. He was very tired. He moved the make-shift cast net pillow and fell asleep on the muddy sand.

In the deadest hour of the night, which is just before the morning star shoulders its way over the eastern horizon, Sprinter awoke to the sound of the old engine of his father's boat and knew that it was as bad as he had guessed it would be. He knew it by one glance at the eastern sky because the star was missing which meant it was still comparatively early.

Pedro stopped the engine a good distance before he reached the beach. The old motor had no reverse gear to act as a brake so he stopped it well out. It had no formal shut down mechanism which still functioned either, so he simply slipped off the fuel line connection and let it run out of gas. He had the distance calculated by plenty of practice. The only pleasant surprise of the night had been that the old machine had started instantly when he recovered the last of his line. Sometimes it would do that when it had cooled off completely. It needed a new water pump among many other things. The last of the momentum pushed the bow of the little boat gently onto the muddy sand.

"No good wasting the bait," Pedro said. The two of them pushed the boat clear out of the water and up onto the shelf of the beach.

They unloaded the boat as carefully and methodically as if it had been a good night. Sprinter hung the lamp on a nail inside the shed where they kept the engine and the lines and the plastic fuel tank. The pails, with the hooks all neatly spaced around their rims, went on a rough wooden shelf. Every item had its special little home in the gear house. Pedro put the lamp out as soon as they closed the door. It was no use burning the kerosene. The faint glow of the lights from the street parallel to the fishing beach was adequate for them. They knew where every stone and crab hole was on this familiar piece of ground.

Two black cars drove slowly along the road where the lights were and stopped adjacent to the beach. Pedro stood at the door of the storeroom. Sprinter had the cast net in his hand to take home with them. He was going to work along the mangroves in the morning to see if anything had changed. He was still young enough to believe in the future and the promise of a new, better day.

Four men got out of one car and five from the other. Three of them took up positions at the entrance point to the short track which led from where the boats were pulled up to its intersection with the roadway. The rest came down to where Pedro and Sprinter were standing, slightly nervous over this sudden influx of visitors so late in the night (or early in the morning, depending on how you looked at it).

Everybody in the party had a rifle. The ones

nearest the street had them in their hands. The group walking toward Pedro and Sprinter carried them slung over their backs except for the one in the lead. He pointed his directly at the two fishermen and said, "Stand apart."

They each took a few steps away from each other.

"Put that down," he said to Sprinter. The boy dropped the net. He had forgotten that he still had it. He had never been in any trouble with police—if that was who they were—in all his life and was very frightened. He was sweating, although the pre-dawn air was chilly. A cold wind was coming in from the open sea, bringing with it the scent of approaching rain.

"Anybody else down here?" the rifleman asked. He was a very tall man. His features were quite sharp. He looked like he had a lot of East Indian in his ancestry. He had on a beret so you could not see his hair.

"No, ossifer," Pedro said. He was still having intermittent trouble speaking after the stroke. Sometimes this handicap would disappear and then reappear suddenly. Under any kind of pressure or tension it tended to be worse. Particularly when he was nervous. It had come out as "ossifer" or, maybe even to a critical ear, as "assifer."

The man swung the rifle, letting go of the barrel and following through with the stroke, holding the butt in his right hand. The steel tube hit Pedro just below the ear. The blow knocked Pedro to his knees. Sprinter took one step forward, but one of the other armed men slapped him across the face so hard that his ears rang. All the others had hand guns drawn by now.

"Are you a criminal?" the rifleman asked of Pedro who was still kneeling, his right hand holding the side of his face where the gun sight had opened the flesh as efficiently, though less neatly, as a knife would have done.

Pedro shook his head. He wasn't going to chance trying to say anything more in case it came out wrong again. Blood dripped from his hand where he held it against the torn skin.

"Are you a dog?" the rifleman asked. A couple of the other men in the party laughed. They knew what was coming.

"Only criminals and dogs have any business being out at this time of night," observed the rifleman. He sounded like a painstaking teacher instructing a slow learner. "If you is a criminal, we know what to do with you. If you is a dog, then you can go on your way. You decide to be a dog? You look like one down there."

A little time passed during which all were silent. The rifleman looked at Sprinter. "You see any boat come in here tonight, boy?"

"No, sir," Sprinter said through the ringing inside his head. He had honestly forgotten the canoe that he had seen a little earlier.

"I wonder if we have a dog and a liar."

"Maybe they got word that we were onto them, sir," one of the others suggested.

"Maybe the dog or the liar told them something." The tall man was not finished. He had a reputation to maintain.

"So, you decide if you is a dog yet?" he asked Pedro.

Pedro nodded. The other option sounded worse.

"All right," the rifleman said. "Let's see you bark. I will tell you when to stop barking."

Sprinter watched with terrified fascination. He would try to forget it afterwards without success. The ringing was still there in his ears, but not loud enough that he could not hear.

"Okay," said the one who had been called sir, putting his rifle back over his shoulder. "You can stop now. You don't sound like such a bad dog. Some other night I will come back down here and see what kind of cat you sound like. Practice up on being a cat till I get back." They went back up to where the black unmarked cars were parked. Then they drove off down the street. At the first intersection they made a turn and were out of sight.

While this had been going on, the morning star had risen and showed intermittently through the scudding clouds. The night was officially nearing its end. A pre-dawn squall was sweeping in from the sea and bringing sharp gusts of wind with it.

Sprinter tried to get his father to stand up. "Get up, Daddy," he said, but Pedro crawled the few feet through the sand and got himself into a sitting position beside his boat. He pressed his back against the old unpainted hull. That's where he had been the last time and he enjoyed, strangely, the familiar feeling. Still, he hoped that the dizzy part from last time was not coming.

After a while, Pedro got up and walked unsteadily home with Sprinter through the faint gray light of the stormy daybreak. All the time the wind was getting stronger, bending the seaside trees inland and blowing loose fragments of garbage across the empty streets. Sprinter spoke quietly to his father a few times, but realized that the damaged jaw made it very difficult for the injured man to answer.

When Pedro got home, he lay down to rest and thought, *I'll be okay. The dizziness didn't come. I just wish Sprinter hadn't seen it. Without the dizziness coming, it will probably be all right.*

Maybe it was because he never did take the medication correctly. The hospital ran out of it all the time. They have it at other places, of course, but they do not give it away in those other places. If you can't buy it, or get it free, then maybe you die like Pedro. Happens all the time. Nobody lives forever.

Sprinter tried to find out where the "special squad" came from on that night and who had been in it. To Sprinter, what had been done was straightforward murder, but Sprinter was young and unsophisticated. He reasoned that somebody must have been in charge and therefore responsible.

He came up against a solid wall of uniformed

silence. They might have been a Kingston-based unit operating outside the knowledge of the local cops who were often compromised by personal relationships within the various communities, particularly in smuggling activities. Nobody seemed to know anything about them. Maybe they worked with something officially called "Special Branch" and they never had to tell anyone what they were doing. That was one of the reasons they were so special. Maybe they were military boys from some murky alliance with overseas agencies. Maybe they were competitive criminals disguised as officers of the law. The corridors of power and double-cross are so twisted that anything might be true.

He gave up after a while. He did not give up completely, but he came to abandon hope of getting to a certain truth. He gave it up as he gave up his father's trade of scraping a living from trying to catch a few of the scattered remains of the last hardy fish populations hanging on in the dubious muddy floor below the deceptively tranquil inshore waters.

He began to exploit his friendship with the watchman at the marina. He felt that there was the possibility of an interesting future there. It was a pocket of wealth compared to his mean surroundings.

After a while, he got to know the captain of the yacht who had talked to him on the night the tall man and his squad had reduced his father to canine status. The captain seemed to think Sprinter was a bright young fellow. He agreed with Sprinter that this fishing business was a waste of time. The captain was a man with interesting ideas. He was always on the lookout for bright new talent.

As a few years passed, the men who fished further out brought little encouragement back with them based on the increasingly depressing results from the shoals offshore.

One very calm day, the crew of a boat working over the Henry Holmes bank got a good look through their water glass at the bottom over a wide area of the ridge. They were shocked at the expanse of bleached white coral they saw and the algae clinging to the staghorns. It was as though the reefs were dying, even out here. Could the current carry disease into the relatively open ocean? It seemed hard to believe, but the dead chalky coral looked like a submarine cemetery. Only the green strands of algae seemed to show any signs of thriving. This type of flora cannot flourish extensively where the coral is healthy. Given time, they are the winding sheet which envelopes the corpse of a reef.

CHAPTER 6

DEFENDING THE COAST

The not-so-new Member of Parliament—halfway through his second term now—rose to speak at the public gathering. He had put on a few pounds as tends to happen with those who prosper. He looked slightly damp in his formal attire. There was a neat little canopy and a small portable wooden deck with a row of metal chairs arranged in a semi-circle. Flags with the ruling party's colors decorated the scene.

Seated on the chairs behind the rostrum were several men dressed, like the Member of Parliament, in suits and ties as though they were in chilly England instead of sweltering Jamaica. Such attire denotes status for historical reasons. It represents a tribute to the colonial past. All politicians in Jamaica agree that colonialism was an evil institution. They say this and then try to look and sound as though they were officials transported from Whitehall.

The women on the stage had it easier, not being quite as constrained by ridiculous custom. The young lady who accompanied the guest of honor—Mr. Akiyama —had every right to look cool. Dressed as she was in the minimum allowable on such a formal occasion, it was hardly surprising that no bead of sweat appeared on her perfect skin.

On display before the raised area was a speed boat on a shining, anodized aluminum trailer with twin Japanese-built outboards mounted on the transom. *Marine Police* was written on both sides of the hull and below that inscription, a note was painted in slightly smaller letters: *Gift of the People of Japan*. The vessel was as sleek and beautifully shaped as Mr. Akiyama's guest. Obviously, Mr. Akiyama was a man who dealt only with lovely things. Just look at his coffee! Not one imperfect grain. Observe his trees—not a single ugly insect bored into his beans. See now, this clean and gleaming craft. Truly, he is a man on the side of the angels.

The Member of Parliament thanked Mr. Akiyama profusely for his efforts in the acquisition of "this marvelous addition to the arsenal of law enforcement in the defense of the coast." He used that exact phrase having written it down the night before. He praised the agreement with the local dealer to provide the pair of one hundred and fifteen horsepower engines with competent and free service for any item covered by the manufacturer's warranty.

"So be careful you don't bend a blade on one of the propellers," he warned, turning to the group of three policemen selected to undergo special training in the use of this jewel of a craft. "That would be your fault. Warranties do not cover carelessness. Now, pay careful attention to the coast guard captain who will be your instructor for the whole of next week. When he is finished, he will issue you with your certificates of competence. I know we can count on you to be rigid in suppressing miscreants committing wrongdoing in our waters.

"There arc many reports of unauthorized activities being carried out by people who think that making an honest living by fishing in our bountiful waters, as their fathers and grandfathers did, is not good enough for them. They ignore the multitude of fish on their doorsteps as though 'Massa God Fish Can Done!' But fishing is hard—though rewarding—work. Too slow for some.

"That's the type of quick-money mentality plaguing our nation. They think they can solve their problems by some shortcut. There is no shortcut in life. Only the right way is our way. Clean and transparent. That's my motto and the motto of my party. Do it right. And do it in the light! No hugging up of criminals for us! That way you can do your duty and never have to hide anything. We are not into the cover-up stonewalling-of-justice business. That is the style of the opposition!"

There was a soft round of polite applause. Most of it from the people on the stage. But it could have been worse; nobody threw anything.

After the address, all those who had attended the gathering, which was open to the public, got a chance to walk as near to the fabulous new vessel as the rope barrier looped around it would allow. Some seemed more interested in it than others.

"Two times one hundred and fifteen is two hundred

and thirty, Fitz," Rocky said. Rocky had known Sprinter from a time when he was so young that his running had not yet earned him the nickname. As children, he had known Sprinter as Fitz, which was short for Fitzroy, Sprinter's real name. Rocky was one of the few people who still called him Fitz and it was a mark of their lifelong friendship.

"Our two hundred is still plenty quicker. Any single engine is faster than two, unless the two motors add up to nearly twice the power. Them would have to put two one hundred and fifty to equal us. Maybe not even then. The foot part, the gear case down in the water, is the problem. The two-engine boat has twice the drag. It have to pull the two gear cases through the water. But, still, it not going to be a slow boat."

Sprinter took a good look at the three prospective uniformed crew members standing at attention beside the boat. These would presumably be in command of the marvelous addition, as the Member of Parliament had indicated. One in particular had spent a few years in a short-lived experiment conducted in one of the many joint military/police cooperative efforts. It was supposed to cross fertilize the two uniformed forces. It had toughened him up a lot. This one had lost whatever normal sense of humor he might have been born with. It could be a problem if that character, whose nickname was "Merciless," got too familiar with his new assignment.

But Sprinter knew that some time must pass before they would become confident enough to do something really stupid. He could count on power, and the effects of it, to produce a certain level of arrogance and finally carelessness. The whole thing was a matter of timing. He had done quite well lately, so he could wait. He knew they were watching him.

Lucy made her way up to him. She wanted to go. She was tired of seeing Sprinter and Rocky making their careful survey of the new boat. She was also tired of seeing Sprinter eyeing Mr. Akiyama's guest. She had little illusions about men or life in general.

She had been with Sprinter ever since the night he had come to the house where her mother had parked her as a little girl before taking off for America, never to return. He had told Lucy that he had enough money to take her away from the sustained drudgery and misery that her wizened grandmother considered to be a proper environment for a Christian female's upbringing.

After Lucy went to live with Sprinter, her grandmother had sent a message that she would burn in hell if she did not return immediately. She had sent a message back saying that she hoped her grandmother was enjoying the hell of doing all of the housework for a change instead of just giving orders. They had not spoken to one another since then.

Lucy and Sprinter got in the front of their little van and Rocky climbed up and sat on an upturned bucket on the floor of the open-backed vehicle. The van only had two seats. She put their little son, Peter, on her lap.

Mr. Akiyama's Mercedes Benz was just driving out. Lucy considered mentioning that Mr. Akiyama's custom designed rims and tires were worth as much as their third-hand van but decided against it. That ought to be obvious to Sprinter with his all-seeing, ambitious, wandering eye.

When they got down to the fisherman's beach, she let Peter climb over her and open the door. He was just four. He liked to do things like that. He followed his father and Rocky down to where the boat was. Lucy went and sat in the shade of a wide-spread sea grape tree. *He's all right, really*, she thought. *All men are like that; even a little success goes to their heads. Look how the boy loves him. He's not a bad father and there are plenty worse. I wish he did something else, but what else could he do? I hope he doesn't do anything foolish. He ought to listen to the captain more, but he has a stubborn streak, a crazy type of jokiness, and likes to do things his way.*

She trusted the captain's judgment. Once, she had heard the captain tell him, "If you do that, you are on your own." She hadn't heard what it was all about, but she had heard those words. Later that night, Sprinter had said, "Who the hell does he think he is?" and she had said, "Listen to him. You just listen to him for a little." She had said it without knowing what it was all about and he never told her.

Sprinter called to her, saying he was going to take Peter for a ride in the boat. He would be right back. He knew she did not like going out in the boat. She had never learned to swim and was afraid. Peter could swim already. He was big for his age.

Sprinter let the little boy stand beside him as they went out of the harbor and down the channel. It was a bright day with gentle wind. Not strong enough yet to raise a white cap. The blue ocean surface sparkled in the brilliant sunshine. Perhaps it was not so sparkling beneath the surface, but the secrets of the sea are well kept like terrible scars masked beneath pretty clothes.

Sprinter gave Rocky the wheel as soon as they were clear of the actual opening and went up to the bow. Rocky slowed the boat and followed the hand signals Sprinter gave him. When they got to the very tip of the reef, they nosed along a few yards past where the bleached-looking dead coral barrier was just a foot or less below the surface. Both of them knew the place well, but it was not a location where anyone went often. Even the optimistic men who set a few small wire traps for the parrotfish which grazed on the algae-draped stone seldom came through here. There was no point when the open channel was quite near.

"See it there?" Sprinter pointed.

Rocky took the boat ahead slowly. There was a deep crack in the reef that was only about fifteen feet wide, but nearly six feet deep in the middle. On either side, the white skeleton teeth of the dead reef grinned at them as the rise and fall of the swell occasionally brought them to within inches of the top.

"You would have to put a little mark on at least one side, Rocky. A white float like they have around the swimming part at the marina. Even if we cut it in half, it could work. We could put it there just before we were going to need it. As long as me could see it, even close by, that would work. Me know the place, all right, but if you never had a little mark it would be very hard to know when to start the turn. In the day is one thing, and going slow is another thing, but going quick and the night is something else."

The boat was drifting slowly along the line of the reef. There was no other significant break anywhere beyond. Not until it curved and changed to flat rock within a few yards of the mangrove. There was a little channel there as well, but only for very shallow draught rowboats.

"Can we go swimming, Daddy?" Peter asked.

"We can stop for a while at the big cay on the way in."

Peter was ecstatic to have this confirmed. He had expected nothing less because he considered his father to be able to provide wonderful things like that on a regular basis. He was quite fond of his mother, too. He would have liked it better if she was as much fun to be with as his father, but that, unfortunately, was not the case. Still, it was very nice to go to sleep close beside her and look, last thing at night, into her dark loving eyes.

The Desperate Cycle

CHAPTER 7

A LITTLE ACCIDENT

When the Member of Parliament heard that there had been a "little accident" involving the marvelous new addition to the arsenal of law enforcement, he decided he would have to deliver a stern lecture immediately to the driver, reminding him about the warning he had issued back at the acceptance ceremony about damaging a propeller. He intended to say that the next time anything like that took place the cost would likely be taken out of the driver's monthly salary. He was not sure if he had the power to order that, but he would try to work it into his reprimand somewhere.

At the police station, the new patrol boat was back on its trailer. The dealer from Kingston was there already

and so was a white-suited officer from the Coast Guard—
not the one who had run the training course. This was a
much more impressive man. That's why he had on a
white uniform. The Navy—which is the Coast Guard in
Jamaica—regard themselves as "the senior service" and
are very conscious of their colonial traditions. So,
perhaps, it is not surprising that the higher in rank you
get, the whiter your appearance ought to be. They were
gathered around the back of the boat and the Member of
Parliament drove right past the front, which looked fine.
When he got to the stern, however, he saw what the
"little" accident involved.

The entire gear case was missing from one of the
engines. Only a broken stump of driveshaft hung down.
The other transmission was still there but had a big hole
punched through it. You could stand beside it and look
inside to where the gears and the propeller shaft were.
The back of the vessel had a jagged crack running across
it just below where the engines were mounted.

The Member of Parliament instinctively knew two
things. First, he knew for certain that, although he was no
special expert in the science of marine surveying, the
entire year's salary of all the drivers combined could not

fix what he was looking at. The second was that this did not look like the sort of problem that would be covered by any warranty.

The Member of Parliament, the dealer and the Coast Guard officer all went inside the hot, dusty station and sat in the office of the senior superintendent. The first question the Member of Parliament asked was where the driver of the boat and his crew were. The superintendent told him that they were both at the hospital.

Only two men had been aboard as the other was on leave. The driver had a broken jaw. He had struck it on the aluminum frame of the windshield. This one had gone to the hospital with two teeth that he had found on the deck clutched in his hand. He said that he had heard that a man in America had suffered the removal of his penis courtesy of his wife and a kitchen knife. He had heard that the missing organ had been located by police on the public highway and was taken to the local medical facility where they had reattached it successfully. So he was going to enquire about tooth replanting. That ought to be much easier.

The other man had a lot of cuts on his legs and feet, inflicted by the dead, but not harmless, coral on which he had stood and tried to push the boat off. It was all broken staghorn and rough-surfaced brain coral out there where they had gone aground at full speed. The algae made it very slippery. They had not been able to refloat it from its solid perch.

In the morning, a passing fisherman had pulled the stranded craft sternways off from where it was still firmly wedged and then towed them to the marina.

The superintendent had received as full a report as they could give before he let them be taken for treatment. You can do that sort of thing to the lower ranks in Jamaica without causing some sort of problem. If the staff doesn't like it then they are free to vent their pent-up rage upon the public to restore their egos.

They confirmed sighting a boat, with no light of any kind, drifting just east of the harbor mouth. It was highly suspicious. Not unreasonable to assume that the vessel was waiting for some contact to unload or receive contraband. Almost certainly some drug-related funny stuff. The patrol had hailed the darkened boat. When they got no immediate reply they tried to switch on the searchlight but it would not come on. That in itself was another peculiar matter.

This morning, they found that one of the wires to the handheld light had been broken. How did that happen? It had worked the night before and the boat had been tied up at the marina ever since. It had been parked as usual directly below one of the big lights after they had come in from the previous evening patrol. Why would a new wire just break like that? They looked at the dealer. He shrugged. Maybe they got so excited they pulled on it extra hard and it broke. That would come under the heading of abuse, clearly not a warrantable matter. These things happen.

According to the report, the police boat had approached carefully. There were stories of smugglers being armed. There were even recent stories of smugglers bringing arms in. When they got a bit nearer, but still too far off to make out precise details, the suspicious craft suddenly took off "like a jet." That was the expression the men used in their account. It headed straight out to sea. The bright white wake was quite clear in the otherwise dark moonless night. They gave chase, confident that they could follow the fugitive and probably overtake it. Certainly, they hoped to positively identify it.

The fleeing boat made a slight turn and they

corrected it to try and stay on its tail, but their boat strayed just a little on the turn and then they were on the reef and the helmsman had a cracked jaw and the engines were still running but not going anywhere and, well, that's where they remained until morning. They had one cell phone, but it had been in a holster on the waist of the one who had gone over the side to try and force the boat free and was full of water. The angle of the boat was so far from horizontal that a lot of seawater had come over the low back and both main batteries were under water so the onboard twelve volt radio mounted on the dashboard was useless.

"That's how it happened, Super. It was a real mess," the operator had said. They had both tried their best to push the boat off and got properly cut above their boots by the razor-edged rocks. While that was going on, one of them had lost a boot and then he really got sliced up.

"And you think a broken jaw is nice, Super? Look how it is swelled up. Look at these teeth! And I couldn't find all of them. Only two. You think they can put them back in?" the injured soul had wailed.

When the fisherman was pulling them off in the morning, they noticed a very small float, really half a float, just a little distance from where it had happened. The fisherman had wanted to cut it off because he said that he could always use one and it was only snagged by a thin trailing line on the edge of the reef, not attached to a trap or anything, so it must have just drifted there and got tangled in the craggy shallows, but they had stopped him. If they had to go back when the incident was being fully investigated it would help to identify the place. The fisherman had said it would probably unknot itself once the day wind came in and drift away, but they insisted that their order be obeyed. Even in their predicament they possessed the establishment of power lurking in the background, so they had prevailed and it might still be there. Maybe.

Everyone looked upset by this whole sequence of events as set out, but to different degrees. The Member of Parliament concluded he would have to pay a personal visit to Mr. Akiyama and see if the people of Japan might be persuaded to extend themselves as far as the additional gift of two new transmissions. Even if that proved possible, there would be the horizontal break across the transom to deal with. He thought that might be fixable within his budget, so he would try. It was embarrassing, but he could handle that. This was a highly visible project and he could always put off cleaning a few drains. Yes, he would definitely go and see Mr. Akiyama. Mr. Akiyama was such a perfect gentleman that he would never make a member of parliament feel uneasy.

The dealer was really quite tranquil, but he assumed a distressed attitude in keeping with the general atmosphere. Either way, he was going to get paid for the labor. Being a government job, it might take months to collect—even years—but he was a young man.

The superintendent was used to equipment like squad cars and other mechanical assets disintegrating under the rough hands of his men, but, naturally, would have preferred if this new vessel had lasted a little longer. So he put on an appropriate, official frown.

The only person in the room who seemed to take it personally was the white-suited officer from the Coast Guard. He was a very tall sharp-featured man. His rank was commander. He had introduced himself as Commander Singh with the emphasis and precision of one who has recently attained new, elevated status. "Do you know how these people will see this?" he asked the superintendent.

The superintendent, whose rank was properly senior superintendent, did not consider that he was under any obligation to discuss public relations with this member of another service, even if that service thought of itself as "senior," and consequently made no reply. He was not even quite certain how this person came to be here in the first place. He could not have cared less what beachfront characters had to say about the current matter. He supposed that was what this pompous specimen, in his blindingly pristine costume and stupid cap, meant by "these people."

The superintendent had one year left before retirement and had more important things to think about. Things like cementing certain existing relationships so as to enable him to live comfortably even when a time came when he was not able to offer official protection where it was necessary. He was going to see the captain over at the marina this evening, and was thinking carefully about their meeting as he always did. He had a lot of faith in the captain.

"They will think it is funny. A big joke. Do you think you can find out who was in the boat that got away? I'm asking you, Super," continued the white-suited Coast

Guard officer. He sounded like he was having trouble concealing the sound of contempt in his voice.

"I will see what I can do. Maybe it has nothing to do with us here. Perhaps they were waiting for contacts from somewhere else," replied the senior superintendent carefully. He had no wish to pick a fight with this person —one never knew where connections to power might lie.

Commander Singh, flicking a microscopic dust particle from his immaculate trousers, stared at the senior superintendent in disgust. He knew what he was looking at. He was looking at a man who had lost his pride, and quite possibly, something more. A disgrace to his uniform.

CHAPTER 8

YOUNG JOYCE AND THE OLD CAPTAIN

Sprinter rang the bell at the main entrance of the marina. Miller, the watchman, came and let him in. The days of crawling through the wire flap were a thing of the past. He had acquired new rights and privileges over time.

The big lights situated on the long head of the T-shaped dock had come on as usual when their sensors recognized the night. Force of habit from bygone times made Sprinter look at each pool of illumination to see if it held any life. A few of the hardy "tough heads" darted about with their usual immunity still intact. It was dead calm. It was dead and calm.

From across the harbor he could see two small dim

lights that came from platform-based bottle lamps. He heard a few loud splashes. That meant there was some poor wretch out there with a gill net strung along the banks of the channel. The two lights would be on each end of the net to warn passing vessels that there was a net stretched between them and to help the setter keep position with it.

The splashes were from a long stick which they called "The Spirit." The name comes from the idea that it will frighten everything, like a ghost. The idea was to travel up and down, parallel to the nylon fence, beating the water with this spirit, which was supposed to induce fish to abandon caution and start rushing, panic stricken in all directions, thus becoming ensnared.

Sprinter hoped that there was sufficient energy left in whatever still lived in this place, which had once been full of fish, even in his short lifetime, and that a few would blunder into the net. That might at least pay for the kerosene oil that the bottle lamps would consume during the hours that the operation would take. What was going on out there in the darkness was sub-subsistence fishing.

He saw a figure coming along the dock. It was quite a figure.

"Hello, Joyce," he said.

"Hi, Sprinter. Go on down. He's on the phone, but he said to tell you to come on board the boat. He looks pissed. More than usual."

"Me don't see you around for a while, Joycie. What you did to your hair?"

"You like it?"

"It look expensive."

"Well, it's not my money."

"Whoever money it is, it suit you, Joycie. Money always did suit you. Where you live now, on the boat or up by the house?"

"The house, man. You think me is some sort of office maid?"

"Chill, Joycie. Me know exactly what you is. You still like swimming? You want to go with me to the cay? The little one. You remember the little one?"

Joyce hesitated. She was young, but not a fool.

"Give me your cell number, Sprinter. Me will call you tomorrow or the next day or sometime when me see how things going. Me will call you soon. Long time me don't go to the little cay. Only small boats like yours can go there, right?"

"Hardly anybody goes there."

"Me remember it."

Sprinter went on along the concrete dock. He climbed down into the open back of the yacht and opened the glass door into the salon without knocking. The captain had a land line telephone on board connected to a plug on the pier. He said something into it and hung up. He then picked up a big tumbler with what looked like straight whiskey in it.

"You was born in a cave?" he asked Sprinter. The captain seemed bent on setting a certain tone for the interview.

"What you mean, Captain?"

"People who live in caves don't know what doors are for. They're for knocking on."

"Sorry, Captain. You want me to go back out and knock?"

"Cut it out, boy," said the captain. Sprinter took that sort of thing from the captain. The captain was getting pretty old and called everyone "boy."

Sprinter thought the captain was looking even more ancient than usual tonight. He was looking puffy and soft and his hair was dropping out. Broken strands were visible on his shoulders. He always wore his peaked cap in the day so you might not notice the thinning so much. *He looks like all them men that think they got it made*, Sprinter thought. Bloated and nervous. Still, he knew an awful lot. But about old things. That must have been what made it so easy with Joyce a while ago.

The captain made it clear that he knew Sprinter was behind the incident with the patrol boat. He wanted to know if any fool could expect something like that to be kept quiet in a place this size. This wasn't some village where they could clam up. There was no village curtain around a town this size where you might successfully keep secrets. This was a big town with many unfriendly ears and watchful eyes.

The captain thought it might still be possible to create some doubt around what had happened. He had just been talking to his friend, the superintendent, and he thought that was possible. Perhaps it could be planted on some guys from down the coast, but, whatever happened, it had been a stupid, unnecessary thing.

"Like a prank. Do you know what a prank is?" the captain asked. "No? It means a joke like kids make. Childish stuff. There are a hundred quiet ways of messing up a boat's engines without pulling a stunt like that. Sugar in the fuel. Even water in it. Drain out the oil from the transmission so that it seizes up; don't try to tear them off like you did. If you just got it to where they had so much trouble with it that they got sick of the damn thing and let it stay tied up, rather than have it break down with them every time they went out, then you don't have to calculate on some hotshot deciding that the pride of the security forces had been assaulted. Because that's what went down." The captain emptied his glass, then went and filled it back up. He did not offer Sprinter a cold beer like he usually did.

"Do you know what is going to happen? I hear this bulldog crackerjack, Commander Singh, has got a proposal to let him have a small cutter and keep it right here along the front of the marina dock. You think that is a nice development? You know what they have on those things? They have night vision gloggles, they got radar, they got radios that talk to helicopters. You think you can run away from helicopters?

"Now, listen, big shot, if you pull anything like that again, you're finished with me. And, more important for you, I'm finished with you if you try. Don't do anything till I can see if we can get this cutter business out of the way. If they don't find anything to do with it, something will happen somewhere else, or some budget cut will come along, and it will sail away into mothballs. Till then, live on your savings. Go fishing. Look after Lucy and the kid. I like the kid. And, by the way, you don't have a clue how lucky you are to have Lucy. I'm a reasonable man, Sprinter. But you gotta understand this is not a joke."

Sprinter listened, feigning respect. He was listening to an old man with jelly for nerves. Past it. He had some influence left, but time would take care of that like it was taking care of him. His old man breathing was audible all through the salon. It rasped like snoring.

While the captain was talking, Sprinter listened to the wheezing and he remembered how it had sounded when that boat hit the tip of the solid stone reef. It had been the sweetest sound he had ever heard. That noise of the hull climbing right up on the top of the crest and the engine racing like it was going all to pieces. Then hearing afterwards that one of them had a busted jaw. Teeth all over the placc. And that dummy, Merciless, talking about getting them screwed back in. You will be able to see what happened to him every time he laughs from now on —if he ever laughs again. It was a joke, all right. But old soft guys who think they have got it all sewed up, might not see the joke so good.

If people were going to know he was behind it then he intended to tell Joyce about it the way it really happened before she heard some other version and thought it was Rocky or somebody else that pulled it off. Now that was something he knew about. Women liked a man who made them laugh. He was thinking about how Joyce looked tonight when he suddenly realized the captain had stopped scolding him. Must have run out of breath. His lungs must be wearing out, too. That was certainly how they sounded: leaky.

"Anything you say, Captain," Sprinter said.

Miller, the watchman, was coming back down the dock. The captain went out through the glass door and spoke to him.

When he came back, he said, "Okay, Sprinter. Get on out. The superintendent is here to see me personally, and I prefer he don't see you on board. Not right now. Go out through that old piece of open fence. It's nothing personal, you know. But I have to get things under control, so stay cool. I always liked you. But you gotta keep cool. Take it easy."

Sprinter climbed back up onto the surface of the finger pier against which the yacht was moored. Looking down from the elevation, he could see the captain's head shining in the glare of the nearest pole-mounted arc light. *All of it's gone off the top*, Sprinter thought. *It looks like a big, wrinkly, scaly golf ball shining in the light.* Lifting up the old flap, Sprinter measured, by eye, the distance from the breach in the fence to the straight, clear front of the marina dock where the threatened cutter would have to dock.

Sixty feet at the most. Not far at all.

The Desperate Cycle

CHAPTER 9

JOYCE ASSISTS IN SPRINTER'S EDUCATION

Mr. Akiyama offered no protest when his secretary, Karen, asked him to let her stay overnight in town rather than trying to drive back in the dark up the doubtful mountain roads. Mr. Akiyama appreciated all the qualities of this excellent, positively overqualified secretary. He could show her off anywhere, unlike some of the others. He had noticed she had been quite a feature at the boat ceremony. Still, like his friend down at the port, who was known as the captain, he was not getting any younger and a night without the possible necessity to prove otherwise was quite welcome nowadays.

In many ways, the real country girls who stayed at home with their mothers in the bamboo-shaded hillsides were so much simpler. In every way, really. But well-spoken, manicured Karen could go anywhere and that was not the case with the others. Still, he missed the tranquility of the gentle easygoing mountain girls. Karen was uncertain in her moods. Almost unstable sometimes. Maybe it was being so far from the bright lights. Perhaps the trip would calm her down a bit. He would not allow her to smoke in the office and she understood that. Nowadays, it seemed like she had to go outdoors for a cigarette all the time. Mr. Akiyama sighed. Only Blue Mountain Coffee was perfect. Everything else was unreliable.

He gave her two of the extra special packets of the absolute best coffee samples to give Joyce for the captain. He knew that Joyce, the captain's secretary/mistress, was fast becoming good friends with Karen. They seemed to have a great deal in common despite the disparity of educational and social background.

This trip was supposed to involve seeing Joyce and arranging some charitable work involving Mr. Akiyama donating a computer to a school in the town. The computer was too old to be worth upgrading to the new system that was being installed at the farm so that was all right. It was not obsolete, just a little slow and old.

The gear case affair was no big deal either. He would be able to easily create the illusion of a complex and difficult negotiation. Since the Member of Parliament wished that there should be no publicity surrounding the whole episode, there would consequently be no advantageous news releases. He would point this out with careful politeness to the Member of Parliament who was now in a position as state minister in a division which dealt with trade and imports. So he should expect no difficulties with chemical products that changed names inexplicably from time to time.

The white coats from the university's environmental faculty were making as much noise as ever, but the time was coming for a reallocation of funds from government grants to that particular department. These academics might have to eventually contemplate staying where they were or going out and getting a real job. In a special place of his heart, Mr. Akiyama had some sympathy for the criticisms that were leveled at his company's use of some of the more lethal pesticides, but his devotion to his duty concerning the production of the crop restrained and strengthened him. The magic of the island's natural beauty was an interference to his dedication, but it was working on him in a subtle way.

His mind returned to considering the situation at hand.

It would be nice if the police boat operators knocked off a gear case regularly so that the excellent developing friendship with this rising and well-connected political star might rest on an increasingly solid foundation. Mr. Akiyama had never been in a position right at the top of an organization at home as he had been for a long time now in this interesting place.

When he had described what he thought were beautiful and ingenious intersections he had created between favors and consequences in Jamaica to a visiting executive from Tokyo, he had been quite surprised when this most eminent person had told him that they were way ahead of him in this field back in the old country. Did Mr. Akiyama not read about how many suicides were linked to discovery of official misconduct in The Land of the Rising Sun? That was due to discovery, of course, not to the corruption itself. Mr. Akiyama disliked the use of the word corruption intensely, but had made no comment. He was tired and looked forward to a good night's rest.

Late the next morning, Sprinter picked Joyce up at a little cove where a path led down from the highway to the sea. She was not alone as he had confidently expected. The knock-out from the presentation ceremony where the patrol boat was being handed over to Merciless and Co. was with her. He wasn't so sure about this new development.

"This is Karen," Joyce said. "She and me, we do lots of stuff together. She has something for you to try." Karen lit a hand-rolled cigarette and took it from her mouth and gave it to Sprinter. He took a drag on it as he backed the boat off the sand. He had smoked weed for years so he knew this was mixed. He had always been suspicious of what was called "seasoned" joints, but he was not going to say that right now.

They passed the main cay where, even on this weekday, there were a few boats and went on out to the little rockbound island to the east. On the way, they passed a sailing boat coming up the channel heading into town. The sails were furled and she was using the engine in the almost calm weather.

The yacht had a yellow quarantine flag showing that it was a vessel arriving from a foreign port and not yet cleared by customs or immigration. A man was steering in the open cockpit and a woman with long blonde hair was standing on the bow holding the forward stay. She looked like she was checking the buoys as they passed to make sure they were centering the approach correctly which would have been a sensible precaution when entering an unfamiliar port. There was an American flag at the stern. The name *Freedom* was painted on the back in pretty, red-bordered gold letters. Karen made some private joke about the name to Joyce and they both laughed.

The "little" cay, as it was called locally, had a very small opening where you could get to the shore. It was like a perfect miniature atoll with a horseshoe reef that almost closed around the island of sand and stone. On the shore, a few sea grape trees grew, somewhat stunted by a rock-choked root system.

There was about five yards of beach. It could only accommodate one boat in comfort and few people bothered with it because of that and the tricky, narrow entrance. No big vessel could moor there. Sprinter took his boat right in, dropped a bow anchor, and tilted the big engine all the way up with the hydraulic lift. He got out of the boat and onto the sand where he could stand. He walked ashore with a stern line and tied it to one of the sea grape trees. Then he pulled the stern close, to within a few feet of the beach. It was early afternoon and the water in the shallows was very warm due to the sun having baked it all morning.

Karen gave him another of her special smokes, and he had less hesitancy this time. Joyce took a big bag with her onto the shore and spread out some beach towels. She had stepped out in about twelve inches of water in the clear sand so she left her sandals in the boat. Karen sat on the front and took the top of her bathing suit off. She was smoking and had a drink in one hand that Joyce had poured for her from a bottle of Appleton Rum. The little cay was so far from the channel that even a Maersk Tanker making its way up the channel behind the white dot of the sailing boat looked small from here.

"You going swimming, Joycie?" Sprinter asked.

"Have a drink with me, Sprinter," Joyce replied.

He took the drink but was less sure about that than even the second special cigarette he'd had. He was not much of a drinker. He liked a cold beer occasionally, but this rum business was something he was hesitant with. He had seen what it did to the night fishermen.

"You making any money these days?" Joyce asked him.

It was becoming a sore point all around. Lucy had been grumbling that Peter should go to the kindergarten school. He was six and everybody said what a bright little boy he was. The van needed two tires and, on top of that, the big outboard engine had started to sound uneven at idle. It needed a set of plugs but they were expensive tipless plugs used in the electronic ignition of some high performance V-6 marine engines.

The newly arrived Coast Guard cutter was in residence since this morning at the marina so he knew the captain didn't even want to scc him, let alone talk about any business. Anyway, he heard that the captain was out of town. Joyce had told him that. But he was not going to tell Joyce that all these stresses were hanging over him. He wanted to tell her the story about the police boat. So he said, "Me got a big thing coming up. Big."

"Me know Captain shut down everything, Sprinter. You think me don't know anything."

"Listen, Joycie, you think me live and die by Captain? You live and die by him? If you do that then what you doing out here now? You and me got to get past them old timers. Don't you know that?" He took her hand and rested it over the zipper of his pants. "Why you bring Karen? Tell me that."

"We do all sorts of things together, me and Karen. Even though she got a big time education and a secretary degree, she is a real sport, boy. You ever did it with two women, Sprinter? Rich people get to do that. You want to pretend you is a rich man today? No problem. But you only get that regular if you is really rich. You only get it regular with girls like me and Karen if you got money. Not if you just say that you is going to be rich tomorrow. That don't work. Even those starve-gut fishermen say that: 'Me is going to catch a whole heap of fish tomorrow'. Catch what? You going to catch flu? Maybe! Sprinter, you want to know something? Me think you is a little scared of the captain because he got you started."

"Me don't take orders from him unless me feel to. You hear about the police boat? Me never asked him nothing at all about that. That was me on my own. You want to hear more about the police boat?" When she agreed, he told her the story. When he was finished, she called Karen over and he told them both the story again, only better. He had remembered more details. Some of them had just occurred to him.

They were drinking all the time. The sun was slanting a little to the west now, but still bright and hot in the cloudless sky. When he had finished telling them the police boat story, they all decided to have a swim in the very warm water. Joyce took off her bathing suit before they went into the placid sea. She was laughing all the time now, even before he had finished the story. "Why get it wet?" she had said as she threw her bathing suit to the side and walked slowly into the clear blue water. It was another joke. It made a lot of sense and was funny at the same time. Particularly, if you had finished the first bottle of rum and were halfway through the second.

Sprinter, Joyce and Karen stayed at the island until it was quite dark and then they all went up to the captain's house in the foothills. Sprinter called Rocky on the cell phone to join them and make the private party last—the more the merrier principle. That was Joyce's idea. It was the first time Sprinter had ever been inside the captain's house. He wondered what it would be like to live somewhere like that without being too old to enjoy it as the captain clearly was. The captain's bed was so large it could not have gotten through the front door of Sprinter's house.

That next morning, Rocky showed Sprinter a revolver. It was a .38 caliber Smith & Wesson Airweight model, originally developed for the FBI, with no tail on the hammer, so that, when you drew it, there was nothing to hitch on any item of clothing. Sprinter asked him where he got it. Rocky said Jinks gave it to him.

Jinks was the leader of a waterfront gang and a man quickly developing a fearful reputation. Sprinter told Rocky that if the police ever caught him with that gun the best he could hope for was to go to prison for life. Look at the erased serial number, for God's sake. More likely, they would just shoot him on the spot and say he went for it. That was the standard story.

It was usually published like this: "A police patrol accosted a man who suddenly pulled out a gun and was killed in the subsequent shootout. Officers deemed to have acted in justifiable self defense." Popular culture believed that the constabulary kept a press release with that printed on it ready at all times. The date and number of attackers killed were filled in as required.

It happened almost every day to the dismay of

Amnesty International and some local human rights groups. These sensitive types had as much following as the impracticals up at the university, and some unrecognized environmentalists who gave speeches about regulating development at all costs. All left wing loonies. "Out of touch with reality," the solid citizens said privately to one another on their wide verandas in the cool evenings.

Sprinter asked Rocky what was going on between him and Jinks. Rocky said Jinks thought the cracking up of the police boat was pretty funny. He said it showed balls. Jinks said a time was coming when this whole harbor was going to be his turf. It was coming fast. The old timers were finished. Some of the police, especially the younger ones, understood that. The Coast Guard was still a problem. Discipline had not quite broken down there yet; people still took that branch of the security forces quite seriously. Jinks would be interested in ideas about that.

Jinks was a street man, a product of the ghetto, with little knowledge about what you could do beyond the limits of dry land, so he had been interested in meeting Rocky after he heard about the boat smash. That is what he had called it: "The Boat Smash."

While Sprinter and Rocky had been talking, they leaned against the railing of the balcony of the house which looked out on the garden and a little stream that sloped down to the sea. You could hear the water as it chuckled over its rocky bed.

Joyce poked her head through the open window. "What's wrong with you guys? You run out of energy? We got to get out of here by mid day. You wasting time. You want us to dry up and blow away?"

Sprinter and Rocky went back inside, but the atmosphere of the morning was not the same as the late evening and night. They told the girls they had to go and "do some business" and were gone. Karen stayed only long enough to have a morning shot of vodka and a cigarette.

Later on, after Joyce had tidied up the place, she sat on the porch in the bright, all revealing light of mid day. Joyce shook her head and was pleased to find that her headache was passing. She was not by nature a worrier, but she was beginning to feel the approach of worry. She had seen how substance abuse had affected others. She had seen it all around her and was beginning to distrust the chemistry of the "seasoned" cigarettes and other things. Seasoned spliffs, as these were called, consisted of blends of marijuana and cocaine or crack.

She knew what they did to her and thought she could handle it. Certainly, it delivered a sense of abandon. Reality receded and "now" became the only thing. She thought of herself as a "now" sort of person, but she was ultimately a survivor, and she knew that some chemicals could be an enemy of survival.

Fear entered her soul as she thought of friends from the streets. Mary dead on the sidewalk. Janet dead. Pearl dead. *Me is going to stop it*, she thought. *Maybe not right now. But soon. Me just want a little security, and me swear, on me mother's grave, me is going to stop it. Me just want to feel safe and then probably me won't need it anymore. God, make me feel safe.*

CHAPTER 10

JINKS AND SPRINTER

Rocky thought about what Sprinter had said about the gun. He went to see Jinks a few days later. He was going to ask him to keep it for him until he organized a safe place to store it. He had thought about saying that, but, at the last minute, he changed his mind and decided he would say "stash it." It sounded more professional.

When he got past the people who were always hanging around Jinks, the surprisingly small, beady-eyed man, who was rapidly carving out a name for himself as the toughest upcoming don around, said the idea showed good sense. It would be available whenever Rocky would need it. Now, he was going to give Rocky something useful, like a reward for this demonstration of good sense. He was going to send him to meet a young foreigner who had been making some enquiries about buying some weed. Apparently, this man had gotten the brush-off from the captain but was still in town.

Jinks told Rocky the name of the man's boat. It was called *Freedom*. He guessed it was at the marina. Jinks wasn't asking anything in exchange for this piece of information. It was a present.

When Rocky got to the dock, the sailing yacht was not alongside. It was out in the deep wide bay to one side of the marina where they put visitors that preferred to stay on the anchor. The daily fee to moor there was a quarter what it was to tie up in a slip where you could connect to electricity, cable, and water. Yet, you still benefited from the security alleged to be provided by being close to the lighted marina and within what they called their "area of control." Most sailing yachts, which tended to have smaller budgets than the cruisers, opted for that.

Unlike the big power vessels, they seldom had air-conditioning, so they enjoyed being able to allow the boat to swing her bow into the prevailing wind. With the forward hatch and portholes open, the fresh cooling wind flowed unimpeded through the boat. This natural ventilation system appealed to these canvas lovers who were all environmentalists. They called vessels, which depended on engines alone, "stink pots."

The people on these sailboats were usually younger types, but not all of them. Aging graduates of the hippie movement turned up frequently; older fellows, tanned to epidermal destruction, and leathery women, many with numerous bits of rustproof shiny metal pinned through a wide variety of locations on their bodies.

One of them once left behind a gleaming, three-inch-long, flat, oblong-shaped ornament, which had become dislodged from its fleshy home during a lively dockside dance session. A boy found it the next morning. He screwed a hook into it and pulled it on a short line behind his tiny rowboat and immediately caught a mackerel with it, thus demonstrating that these objects were attractive to fish as well as those who considered stainless steel decorative and alluring.

The boy kept this secret fishing weapon hidden for months in case the owner discovered that it was still around and had not been lost in the murky harbor water. This young fisherman had never been able to afford a real "spoon" lure in all his life. He had constructed homemade versions from pieces of old chrome motorcar bumpers, but this was becoming hard to find in these days of plastic. This new invention was much better. He was terribly distressed one day when a big fish grabbed it, snapped the line, and went away with the jewel. The boy hoped fervently that another piece of similar body enhancing armor would drop off again at some time in the future from another abandoned reveler and that he would be lucky enough to find it.

Freedom's crew was part of the young brigade. When Rocky rowed out to them in a borrowed dinghy, the man was drinking a Red Stripe beer and he offered Rocky one. The woman was sunbathing, lying face down on the front. Her long blonde hair was spread out on the deck.

"Hi," the man said, "I'm Curtis." Curtis was quite frank with Rocky. He and his girlfriend knew a few couples who financed endless cruising through the Bahamas and the Antilles by purchasing relatively small amounts of drugs and taking them into South Florida. They would make three trips a year at most and the quantities were insignificant enough that they did not disrupt the big established importers. To do anything grander might draw attention and lead to the organized cartels turning them in to stifle competition while, at the same time, earning points for their friends among compromised authorities in the Florida Keys or Miami. It was a relatively low-risk lifestyle as long as you kept it small enough to stay beneath the radar.

It was safer now than ever with the United States Coast Guard under pressure to do their part in foreign wars. There was only so much funding. Folks of the kind who drifted peacefully from island to island practicing this unapproved career in the exquisite water garden of the Caribbean were generally disapproving of military expansionism on the part of the American Government, but they recognized that it had some pleasant side effects.

This couple had come here once before and got a few kilos from the captain, so were disappointed when the old man had said that everything was on hold for the moment. They heard it was wide open in Haiti with territorial warlords running that island of misery, but Curtis had never been there and was afraid of the language barrier. They had not totally given up yet. They made a few discrete enquiries and were staying on for a week or so, depending on what turned up.

If it really was hopeless, they would continue west and try Montego Bay or Negril. Many said Negril was the best place, but they had never been there and it is always nice to be in comparatively familiar surroundings.

The sum they had to spend was still big enough to sound impressive to Rocky who was used to what trickled down to him via Sprinter after the captain decided what he could spare. He had talked to Sprinter before he came out to the sailing yacht and the amount was twice what they had decided was worth defying the captain's orders to take a vacation.

Rocky said that he would bring Sprinter to meet them and talk about the details because he had never done anything without his partner. His partner Fitz. He made it sound like Sprinter and he were equal in everything. It had not been like that all the time, but that was how it seemed to be turning out. The party with the girls had helped to equalize them.

Sprinter and Rocky decided to row over to *Freedom* after dark to work out the final details of the transaction. Nothing would be handled inside the harbor. *Freedom* would clear for the high seas rather than a specific destination and they would meet a few miles offshore. It was a routine type of handover in every way except that it was the first time that Sprinter had ever handled a shipment without the captain's blessing.

On this occasion, they did not go to the marina but used a little, leaky wooden rowboat fashioned from unplaned planks. This battered tub was owned by an ancient man who daily scoured the roots of the mangroves for oysters whose shells he had to wipe with solvent and then wash again in seawater to remove the little globs of bunker C oil which stuck to them.

There was no formal stance either for or against the sale for human consumption of these water-filtering mollusks. Considering what poured constantly out of the gullies and pipes and rivers into the semi-enclosed harbor, that may seem surprising until one remembered that the acknowledgement of this pollution was avoided vehemently at all official levels. The tourist board motto was "Jamaica, No Problem!"

On the way back, they rowed quietly past the Coast Guard cutter now positioned along the head of the main dock. In addition to the marina lights, she had a lot of lights of her own. Only the bridge was dark. But in the faint general glow, you could see that there were at least two people up there.

There was only a pair of mooring lines holding the Coast Guard vessel—a bow and a stern connection. No spring line ropes were rigged. You could get away with that as long as the wind was light, as it usually was at night, so if you kept a watch it was okay, given that there is no appreciable tidal flow in Jamaica. Nonetheless, it is not the normal arrangement for a vessel unless an imminent departure is anticipated.

The two men in the row boat took notice of this. It suggested that the cutter was manned for an instant cast off which explained the darkened bridge and, almost certainly, staff of command level inside.

A very tall man in a sparkling white uniform stepped out of the small wing of the bridge and climbed the few steps down the ladder to the deck on the seaward side of the cutter. Rocky was rowing and he pulled on one side to open the distance. Sprinter, feeling content that the darkness protected him, continued studying the opposition. He looked at the man in the semi-illuminated area and wondered if it could be true.

"You think it really is him?" Rocky asked Sprinter as they pushed the oyster man's craft up on the two rollers that were its cradle.

"Me don't know. It was a long time ago and after him hit the old man me never did look at him. Me never did want to look at it." He could have said that more than anything else he didn't want to *hear* it, but he had never told anyone, not even Rocky, about the other part.

"Fitz, if it's him, we can kill him. Jinks can work it out. He's only a man in a white suit. Maybe that's what we should do anyway. If you is even nearly sure then that's good enough."

Sprinter looked at his boyhood friend and knew that this was a new Rocky emerging before his eyes. Something was happening to him. Sprinter knew that a time was coming when he would have to ease away from Rocky. Sprinter could kill a boat or break a man's jaw, but he knew that final step involving murder was beyond him.

The patrol boat prank, as the captain had called it, was his type of undertaking. This talk about killing somebody—anybody—was a leap too far for him. That was no joke at all. Anyway, he had a plan that involved Rocky's help and he hoped that it would appeal to his pal. Look at how the other one they had pulled off was becoming a legend already. If you ever killed a man you would have to live with it and hug it up inside you. You couldn't laugh about it and have a party with a girl and chat about it. Maybe there were people who could and maybe there were girls who would enjoy that, but he was not in that sort of circle. He did not think fun-loving Joyce was either, let alone low-key Lucy, who was talking about making peace with her grandmother and going back to church.

"You can't kill a Coast Guard captain, Rocky. Take that out of your mind. Jinks got you crazy. He's sort of crazy himself, so me hear. That's what everybody say about him and him is getting you crazy, too. Listen to me now. You know where you can get two air tanks to borrow? Scuba tanks. You know any of the divers that would lend you two for a few hours? How far you can swim nowadays? You was a big time swimmer."

That was true. His nickname, "Rocky," came from his using big stones to help him go deep when he was free diving as a youngster. Sprinter saw Rocky coming down from the excitement that had arisen from the crazy wild talk about murdering the tall man on the cutter. He went on, speaking quietly and calmly to him about other things and saw him getting back to normal and looking more like the old, solid Rocky.

The grizzled oyster man came up, interrupted them, and asked sternly where the money for the rent of his ruin of a boat was. They told him he would have to wait a few days. He was very annoyed. He sounded like the owner of a chartered cruiser who had been told that the contracting party was waiting for funds to be transferred to a numbered bank account and was experiencing difficulties.

He made them understand that future requisitioning of the skiff would be on a strictly cash-up-front basis. He went off grumbling, saying that he intended to inspect the hull carefully in the daylight tomorrow to make sure there were no scratches or other damage and if there was such injury, whether cosmetic or structural, then additional charges would have to be paid before any new lease agreements could be enacted.

Over at the marina, the captain had seen the little craft come and go from the side of *Freedom*. The distance was too far to see who was in it, but he had watched it head off in the direction of the commercial fishing beach. He called Miller, the watchman, and gave him some money and told him to go over and try to find out who was in it. There were not many boats moving around so that ought to be quite simple.

Commander Singh came over and introduced himself formally to the captain. He was pleased to meet a senior member of the management committee of the marina. Did the captain live aboard? No? But he obviously spent much time on this beautifully maintained vintage vessel. If he ever noticed anything that seemed suspicious would he let him know? Surely, his years in the location gave him much local knowledge.

"And may I present myself, miss? I am Commander Singh."

Joyce looked him over, liking the neat white uniform and his sharp features. She often stayed late at the marina, keeping the interior of the captain's yacht in Bristol condition.

She asked Commander Singh if he stayed aboard the Coast Guard cutter and he said most of the time, but that he also had a room at the nearby hotel. He said this was provided to accommodate occasions when he might have to meet privately with confidential sources or high officials of the state. All of that sounded most impressive to Joyce. She understood that as an agent of law enforcement he might have reservations about homemade cigarettes—seasoned or otherwise—but noticed that he drank the captain's whiskey enthusiastically. That was a good sign.

After Commander Singh left, Miller came back and spoke quietly to the captain. The old man shook his head, then thanked the watchman. *Well*, he thought, *I tried explaining the situation to him.*

The Desperate Cycle

CHAPTER 11

THE COAST GUARD CUTTER MAKES A VERY SHORT VOYAGE

The *Freedom* cleared for departure at four in the afternoon and proceeded out from the headland that sheltered the windward side of the harbor entrance. She had her sails up as soon as she opened sufficient space to tack to the west in the dying sea breeze. From inside you could see her for about fifteen minutes then the land got in the way.

Commander Singh sat in the wheelhouse of the cutter with his first mate. "Nothing is going to happen till after dark," he said. They both had night vision glasses on the chart table. There was no visible sign that there was any particular alert on board the cutter. They had not moved from the dock for two days so the impression was being created that there was some loss of enthusiasm in their level of vigilance. Everything was not just normal, but a little sub-normal.

The night came on. The sea wind was falling out rapidly now and shifting very gradually as it prepared to follow the regular pattern of island weather. Soon, it would come from the already rapidly cooling land. When it was fully dark, Sprinter eased up the old familiar flap in the chain-link fencing and held it clear for Rocky's solid, compact body to go through.

They took a careful look around before Rocky waded into the water. Sprinter paid out the light rope as Rocky moved away from the shore. He could only proceed ten feet out into the dredged basin before he was in water too deep to stand. After a while, Sprinter no longer could detect any outward pressure on the line and he cut it, looped it and tied it with a bowline knot to a chain.

Sprinter watched the chain begin to slide steadily off the shore until it was all gone. He went back through the flap and secured it. Rocky would swim past the fence when he was coming back and arrive at the shore halfway between the perimeter fence and the fishing beach. Rocky had argued that the whole delivery job of the small consignment of marijuana would have been better done somewhere down the coast if it was really a matter of money, but Sprinter had appealed to his sense of adventure.

This was going to be the big event that would mark them as beyond the control and oppression of anybody in the port. "You want Jinks to respect you, Rocky," Sprinter had said. "See what happens when he hears about this. This is the real thing. This is not outboard engine business. They going to howl like a dog when we finish with them—the captain as well as that son of a bitch coolie bastard up there in the bridge of his warship. Either way, it works out. If they do what me think them is going to do, then it is perfect. If them just sleep and let us go through then we still don't lose and maybe they get in trouble when they try something next day or whenever. It won't be as big a joke, but it won't be bad either."

Sprinter had got brand new sparking plugs for his engine. Well, almost brand new. A friendly policeman had taken six of them from the hardly-used patrol boat engines that were waiting for the anticipated gifts from Mr. Akiyama before they could go anywhere. He had replaced them with the worn out ones from Sprinter's motor. That was another little triumph.

They put everything that they were to hand over to Curtis in Sprinter's boat, then called Curtis on a cell phone. *Freedom* was drifting under bare poles just off the northeast point. Curtis reported that there was not much wind outside, but that he could smell the land, indicating that the breeze was being pushed out by the cool fragrant air flowing off the mountains. It would be coming all the way from the damp chilly peaks where the Blue Mountain Coffee grew.

"That's them," Commander Singh said. He had the infrared sensitive glasses to his eyes and saw Sprinter's boat pulling away from the beach. The mate spoke to a runner at his side and the man set off to give the orders to let the lines go. Commander Singh had both of the cutter's high-speed diesels running in neutral. He could see the bow line come aboard. The mate was leaning out the window, tightly controlled in his excitement. He motioned to indicate that the stern was free.

Commander Singh put the engine on the seaward side astern to bring the bow slightly off the wharf. The mate had the glasses now. The cutter shuddered strangely but the bow had come a little away from the dockside, the gap opening by the second. Commander Singh slipped the other engine into forward and put a little power on her. The engine that had been in reverse stopped suddenly and the one that had just gone in gear made a loud growling noise and stopped as well. The land breeze was drifting the cutter away from the dock all the time, bringing the bow more and more out into the clear.

Commander Singh put both motors in neutral and restarted them. They sounded perfect. The cutter was being blown out into the basin by a freshening wind off the land. She was so far away from the T-head that there was no further need for maneuvering. The commander put both engines in forward and put the throttles firmly ahead.

Inside his brightly lit salon, enjoying his regular evening cocktail on his yacht, the captain could hear the grinding clatter that not even four feet of shrouding water could totally muffle. He had been a seaman for more than half a century and knew that was the sound of a major mechanical disaster. He jumped up from his easy chair, almost spilling his drink, and actually ran out into the stern where he could see what was happening. It was the fastest he had moved in years.

Halfway across the dredged marina he could see the cutter dead in the water. He could hear some orders being shouted, but could not make out the precise nature of the commands. They had the contradictory sound of uncertainty in them. He thought he heard the word anchor once then a voice saying to wait.

They were running out of sea room between where the bank of the shallow edge projecting from the shore formed a natural breakwater. That was why the owners had sited the marina here in the first place. The nose-shaped bar provided shelter from the strong northwest winds of the winter months.

The captain, now standing in the open cockpit of his yacht, watching with fascination, heard the engines start once more. Then he could see that the vessel was aground on the mud bank and there was a lot more shouting. He went back inside through the glass door and sat back down. Nothing life threatening could happen to them where they were, and he certainly did not have the kind of power to draw the cutter off with his yacht. Especially off mud. This material creates a giant suction cup along the side and bottom of a stranded ship and sucks it to itself.

The hardest job in refloating a grounded boat is when mud takes hold of her. Rock tears you, but is usually prepared to set you free. Torn, but free. The embrace of sand is like that of a casual lover. Not mud. Mud makes you almost a part of her. Only the terminally enveloping grasp of quicksand is tighter.

He considered carefully and smiled an old man's smile. *You have to hand it to that boy*, he thought. He did not harbor the slightest doubt that this was his one-time protégée's handiwork. He looked forward to discovering exactly what had been done. He had been young once himself, as they say. Life was certainly interesting. He had felt badly about giving Singh information about the *Freedom* and the visit of his rebellious ex-employee, but now it was just a matter of intense interest to him in seeing how it evolved.

Joyce came out of the forward cabin. She was brushing her hair. She had been asleep. "What's going on?" she asked. There was developing commotion on the dock as some of the crew from the Coast Guard boat had been still ashore when she pulled out.

"Your handsome, straight-haired commander has

got himself into an awkward situation. It seems that his beautiful suit was not sufficient to keep him out of difficulties. Try not to laugh about it in his presence. I do not think he will take this lightly." The captain enjoyed giving her this news. He was certainly getting old, but, though he was suffering other major deterioration, his eyes worked quite well.

The next day, while waiting for the port authority's biggest tug to get over and free the cutter of the embracing mud, they had a diver go underneath so as to determine exactly how solidly she was grounded and inspect the propellers, rudders and shafts. When the man got back from his explorations, he took off his mask and tried not to look amused. He was a Coast Guard diver and had to take his career into account.

He described how the two propellers had been shackled to one another with chain so each became, in practice, the deadly enemy of the other. Once the gear train engaged, they imposed such a load that the engines would stop. There were a few local people on the wharf employed to the marina or doing odd jobs on docked yachts, and, before evening, the story was widely known, although exactly who leaked it in detail was a mystery.

Commander Singh was extraordinarily controlled. He issued only the most reasonable and practical of instructions and appeared almost detached. He was assuming a position above the situation. The captain spoke to him during the day and they agreed that it was a criminal assault on the state. It would be impossible for the perpetrators of an act of this type to remain anonymous for long. Certainly, it had all the hallmarks of the now-famous patrol boat incident. Normal investigations would proceed.

There was not very much damage to the cutter as far as could be ascertained at this stage. Although the soft mud held her close, it would not hurt anything seriously and even the propellers showed only minor abrasions. The big shafts were far too heavy to bend under that pressure. The port authority would charge a lot for the deployment of their largest tug, but they comprised another arm of government so they would have to join the lengthy queue of interdepartmental creditors.

Everyone directly concerned maintained a studious avoidance of the central issue which was the perception that a comedy of significant proportions had been staged and would join the ranks of waterfront tales, growing to epic proportions as time passed. It would take something quite spectacular to stop that.

The big twin-engined tug arrived too late to allow the salvage to be carried out in daylight. The cutter rested peacefully for one more night on the soft bed of mud.

In the calm of the usual brilliant morning, the salvage team set a stern anchor on the cutter to stop the back from pivoting any further on top of the shallow bar and the tug pulled the bow gently free. They took up the slack on the stern anchor and hauled it up. Once the tugboat captain had her in the deep, open turning basin, he took his tow line off and the cutter re-anchored in the clear and swung head to the wind. They did not even bring her back to the dock where a number of spectators were gathered watching the professional behavior of established, competent authority. The diver went back over and cleared the chain. They hauled it aboard after he secured one end to a light rope.

This was done as discretely as possible on the side away from the watching crowd where there was quite enough vulgar hilarity to be observed already. After that, they started the two engines. Commander Singh let the mate take her out through the channel, following the tug down through the fairway. He had informed the management of the marina that they would be proceeding to Kingston where a survey would be done to determine that no major harm had been suffered. He made the whole matter sound almost routine.

Joyce stood on the pier among other witnesses to this departure. She laughed with her pretty friend Kelly from the marina office who thought Joyce was a great success and loved being with her. Both of them had glasses of ice and vodka, and Joyce was smoking a cigarette. They were girls who liked to have fun.

"If that boat was a dog, Kelly, it would have its tail between its legs," Joyce said. "Me going to let you meet the guy who did that. Me going to ask him to take you and me swimming one afternoon and let him tell us how he worked it. That boy have a big future. They called him Sprinter from when he was a little boy, but you know what him is today? Him is a silver bullet."

A man standing nearby spoke to her. "You know the guy who did it?"

Joyce looked at him. Her eyes were bright in her smooth, beautiful, dark face. "Know him? Me know all about him. Him is a special friend to me."

"I would like to shake his hand," said the man. "I would like to shake the hand of the man who did that."

Joyce, who spent a lot of time at the marina, looked at the man a little more carefully. "Didn't me see you on that boat? Don't you is one of the crew? On the Coast Guard boat?"

"Yes, they left me here to clear up some things. I have to drive one of the cars back. That's why I get to stay and not have to spend four hours on that boat with that fool of a commander. But I loved to see that. I hope they kick that son of a bitch, miserable petty dictator Singh out of the service for not keeping a proper watch or something. I tell you, I would like to shake the hand of the man who did that."

He was smiling at Joyce while he talked to her. She thought he had a very nice smile. A nice smile went a long way with Joyce.

"Me don't know if him would do that. Him is a big man in this town. And him is going to be bigger. Me and him have a special thing."

"Well," said the man smiling even more brightly into Joyce's wide set dancing eyes, "come and have a drink with me up at the marina bar. You can tell me all about him. He sounds like somebody very special. I hope that miserable asshole Singh commits suicide."

The Desperate Cycle

CHAPTER 12

LUCY MOVES ON AND SPRINTER MOVES UP

It had certainly gone very well. At least that was how Sprinter regarded his latest assault on authority.

Sprinter thought Lucy would have been very impressed with the "Battle of the Crippled Cutter." Unfortunately, she did not seem to appreciate the neatness and perfection of the triumph. He was coming to the conclusion that Lucy was not really quite up to his standard of what women should be all about. She was beginning to remind him of his old schoolmistress who used to look at him disapprovingly through scratched eyeglasses. It seemed to Sprinter that Lucy was losing all her sense of humor.

He asked her what she was going to do with the

money he had given her from the deal with Curtis on the *Freedom* and she said she owed people and had already used some of it to pay them off. She owed Mr. Chin at the supermarket plenty. Other people, too, who had helped them when it was really hard to make ends meet. Now, she was going to put the rest of it down for school stuff that Peter was going to need at the little school.

The next day, Lucy had two boxes and a suitcase packed. She told Sprinter that she was taking Peter to go and stay "for a little time" with the old Christian grandmother.

She said it was time the boy got to know his great granny. The other thing worrying her was that she was getting seriously afraid about a few things. Sprinter should understand that. She said that people told her that Rocky was a part of Jinks' gang and that was a murderous crowd. Then there was the possibility that the big triumph that Sprinter was so proud of having orchestrated was going to bring some sort of new, real danger to them. She did not believe that the forces of law and order were in such retreat that they would just take that lying down. Not for long, and certainly not forever.

Sprinter did not offer any real opposition to her idea

of going back to her grandmother. That was sort of okay with him. Especially when she said he could come and take Peter swimming in the day or for a drive or other things like that—as long as it was in the day. She was very specific that it must be in the daytime.

So it was very amicable and reasonable. He drove Lucy over to the old lady's house which was in the high forested country above town. After dropping her and Peter off, he picked up Rocky who was taking him to see Jinks that morning.

Sprinter had known Jinks from a distance, but over the last few years the little man—who had been called "Shorty" before he insisted on "Jinks"—had functioned in the real underworld of truly ruthless criminals who held small geographical fractions of the town in a grip that was only challenged in any realistic sense by other competitors of equal ferocity. It was a different scene to the almost gentlemanly, however unorthodox, environment that the captain had created within his area of influence and which had sheltered Sprinter.

The street where Jinks ruled was technically a public thoroughfare, but had ceased to function as such for some time. It was a lane connecting two mean streets, but Jinks' men had effectively sealed it off at each end to unauthorized traffic by a loosely assembled, forbidding human cordon. In times of true gangland strife, the sealing was reinforced by dragging out old deep freezers and tires and other debris to block access completely.

In truly major occasions of conflict, when absolute privacy and security were required, the tires would be set afire in the grand traditions of the French street barricade.

Jinks' scruffy honor guard escorted Rocky and Sprinter to where Jinks held court in a sort of sidewalk office comprised of a few chairs and tables right out in the open of this gangland colony. People were standing, leaning or sitting around smoking ganja quite openly. Some were drinking beer or stout, as well as smoking ganja, and there was a domino game going on. It had some of the atmosphere of a casual party about it, including a lot of loud laughter. In the immediate vicinity of Jinks himself, it was much quieter and more businesslike.

There were a few formal exchanges before Sprinter was given a proposal. The waterfront was generally less tightly controlled than the ghetto enclaves. A lot of private initiative was still permitted with crossover types who were genuine fishermen a lot of the time, but were enrolled to provide support where boats were involved. In Jinks' view, it was high time this situation be brought under better management.

Take the case of this old foreigner known as the captain. He had been around a long time. Where did some fat white derelict get off giving orders and setting up schemes? One of the first orders of business would be to tell him to go home. That would be the way. Make him understand that he'd had a good long run. Start up his boat and sail away. Or go and live in his house on the hill and fade out. His withdrawal would create a small vacuum which was desirable in itself, but, more important, it would send a very clear message and the man who delivered it would gain advantage and prestige.

Jinks hoped that the move to tie up the beach would not precipitate some showdown with other up-and-coming dons, as the local gang leaders were known. He always preferred the peaceful route where possible these days since his reputation had already been established.

Naturally, he would spread the word that it was a preference that would be backed up with whatever it took to enforce adequately. He was proposing that Sprinter and

Rocky be his organizers and standard bearers for this ambitious expansion and did they think they could handle it? That was the way he put it. It was a question. "Do you think you can handle it?" He did not ask them if they were interested. That was taken for granted. That was the partial compliment he was paying. It was understood that he was not a man who paid compliments, however backhanded they might be, frequently or casually.

Standing there in the hot street, the smell of flagrant illegality wafting around them, Rocky and Sprinter could see what a future like this could mean. They knew that although Jinks spent some time here in the harsh grubby corner of the world where he had come from, he did so because it was his power base. He drove a BMW. He lived in the cool foothills. You could not even see his house from the road behind the tall trees. They were young and confident.

Sprinter spoke directly to Jinks, determined to establish, right at the very beginning, exactly who was going to make the final decisions when it got to that stage. He was carefully positioning Rocky as a trusted lieutenant—not a divisional commander. "Give me a number where me can call you later today."

He did not make it sound like he was going to call after he had thought about the question Jinks had just asked him. Being able to "handle it" was not a matter ever to be in dispute. He was taking the very slight risk of showing a small amount of disrespect by ignoring the question with the air that it was beneath him and did not require an answer.

He was already trying to convey the impression that, even if he went forth to represent superior force, he went with a certain degree of personal freedom. He would proceed as a senior officer might do following amiable consultation with the chief of staff. That characteristic had got him this far. When he had said, With his statement, he had conveyed that he would call to report how he had "handled it." Jinks had only nodded when he said it, so Sprinter was satisfied that there was a good understanding between them already.

He had made up his mind when he had finally decided to go his way in spite of the captain's directive, that they would have to kill him to destroy his independence. When he had put away all of his father's lines and tackle and abandoned the desperate scrounging life of an inshore fisherman, he had determined to end the cycle of trying and failing at playing by the rules. He knew not from whence came the illness which afflicted the waters. Or who decided to send a party of brutal uniformed oppressors to vent their boredom or annoyance on people crippled by circumstance or illness. He had decided to make up his own rules dealing with things that he felt he could control. And he wanted to have fun whenever possible.

CHAPTER 13

GOODBYE TO ALL THAT

Somewhat to Sprinter's surprise, the session with the captain was not as satisfying as he had anticipated. The older man had listened as though he was receiving an expected message. In the end, the younger man had put it to his ex-boss that change was coming and the wise thing for anybody not connected to the new power to do would be to make room for the shift.

Clearly, the best way of showing understanding was to get out of the way. Probably he, Sprinter, could try and work something out to convince the new order that the captain was out of business but could stay on. This was not a promise. There no certainty that any absolute safety was guaranteed. A time might be coming when it would get mighty hot around the seafront and if there was the slightest hint that someone was an "informer," anything was liable to happen.

He told the captain face to face that he suspected the special attention he had received might have come from feeding information back to the authorities by the captain himself after he had dared to ignore the order to "cool out." The captain was still enough of a man not to make any argument about that, and Sprinter knew that he had been right.

"Listen, my boy," the captain said. "I'm going to get the hell out of here. I know I'm a leftover in many ways. I've been thinking about it for a while anyway. I'm not so much afraid as tired. Maybe it's more than that, too. I wish you luck because you're going to need a big load of it. You think you can take on anything, but you don't have a clue what it's going to be like.

"You ever see that Jamaican movie *The Harder They Come*? That's a joke to what is really on its way down here and you're welcome to it. Remember the last thing I said to you when you came here after you cracked up the police boat? I told you to look after Lucy and the kid. I told you I liked you. Well, remember what I'm telling you this time. You're going to need a load of luck."

Sprinter took one last hard look at the captain and said, "If you stick around you going to need it more than me," and walked out of the salon. He shut the door behind him before the captain could make his old joke about people who live in caves forgetting about doors. *No more of that from you*, he thought.

Sprinter called Jinks and said that he had "handled it." The old fellow was not going to give any trouble. That's how he took care of business. Jinks just said, "Okay," and hung up.

Joyce called Sprinter the next day and he met her at a local bar. "Me got to thank you for something, Sprinter," she said. "Captain told me that you come around to the boat and tell him that the best thing for him is to check out. Said you give him some kind of warning. Then him said that that's fine because the whole place is going to hell anyway. Then you know what he said? He said we is going to get married and he is planning to take me to America and right away. Well, nearly right away.

"So, Sprinter, this girl is going to show you how grateful she is for as much time as we got left. Imagine! Me in America! Legal, too. How long can he live, anyway? If me put me mind to it me bet you me can give him a heart attack in less than a year. Six months, maybe. Go get the boat and let's go swimming. Me love you, boy!"

Going out to the little cay, Joyce was happy, laughing and promising all sorts of ways she was going to demonstrate her gratitude in the limited immediate future. She had her special cigarettes with her and looked like she had been at them while she was waiting in the little cove where he picked her up.

Sprinter, driving the boat and smoking one himself now, was wondering how difficult it would be to try and get Karen's number out of her without spoiling the atmosphere. It had been careless of him not to have obtained that useful information for future use when he had the opportunity. It just showed how you should always be prepared for the uncertainties of life. Karen had a lot of the class and education that Joyce lacked, but, as Joyce had said, she was a sporting girl.

CHAPTER 14

THE CAPTAIN SPEAKS

It was a wonderful trip. Knowing now, what I only suspected with good reason back then, I'm really glad that I did it when I could still enjoy it. Poor old Sprinter. I wonder what they will do with him. None of my business any longer. No more problems for me. Only the big one that we all have to deal with eventually, one way or another. But it was a wonderful trip.

All the way up to Inagua, the Windward Passage was calm and the only event that interrupted us was when a United States Coast Guard ship out of Guantanamo Bay stopped us twelve miles east of Cape Maisi on the tip of Cuba that points toward Haiti. They called us on channel sixteen and went through all their usual formalities. "Please shift and answer channel twenty-two alpha." Has anybody ever seen a VHF radio with twenty-two alpha written on it? I only know it as twenty-two. But that's the military way.

They requested—I love that word—permission to board us for a "routine inspection." A party of five came bouncing over in a Zodiac under the command of a pink young ensign with the obligatory crew cut.

I stopped my boat and let her roll broadside when they came aboard. The kid requested—that word again—that I keep her going ahead, but I said, untruthfully, that Joyce was not capable of steering her and the auto pilot was broken—although it wasn't—and I was not prepared to have the inspection done in my absence so they had to put up with it.

It was calm, but the good old Windward Passage swell never lets you down. The light breeze brought the exhaust fumes into the cabin area. She's an old boat, so they had to go down below in the boiling hot engine room to verify the numbers on the main beam, and the ensign took one whiff of it and stepped back when they opened the hatches.

He ordered some other unfortunate, who had to do what he was told, to go down the stairway and write them up. I could hear him throwing up down below from where we were inside the salon. I asked the ensign who did he think was supposed to clean that mess up and he said, "Not me," and they got the hell back in their rubber boat and hightailed it back to their ship.

They had to come back a few minutes later to retrieve a handheld radio they had left in their big hurry. I never had any use for them, but that is not the popular opinion. I understand that. I suppose I was affected by the game that I got involved with. I am sure there are lots of good fellows in that service. I just never met any. But, after all, I was the competition for a long time. Now, I don't have enough time left to get to like them. I don't like traffic police either, but there must be some first class fellows in that racket, too.

We only stopped at Matthew Town, Inagua for fuel and one good night's sleep after the almost three hundred mile run from Jamaica. It was comfortable with the boat tied up and well fendered against the big concrete commercial wharf that they have in Inagua harbor where they blasted the rock out and made a little artificial harbor. It's the only ugly island in the Bahamas that I ever saw. And the only one where the inhabitants are less than completely friendly.

Everybody either works for the Morton Salt Company, where they extract tons of sea salt from the huge solar drying pans on the north end and pile it up in snow-like mountains, or they do nothing. Well, that's not quite true. Some guys transship illegal people and other things mainly out of bases in nearby Haiti. Others are placed there by various law enforcement agencies to catch these transshippers and then generally make deals with them to allow the activity to proceed for a fee. That's how it works.

The only pretty thing on the whole flat rocky place is a lake in the middle with a huge flock of flamingos. They say it's the largest group of those long-legged pink birds in the hemisphere, but I don't know if that's a fact. They don't have a lot to boast about on Inagua, so they tell you that about the flamingos, which are certainly very plentiful.

Even if they don't have the largest flock of flamingos in the New World, they definitely have the largest flock of mosquitoes. When you open the boat up in the morning, sometimes you have to sweep them up into little black piles where they kamikazed themselves.

Inagua is genuinely famous for salt, flamingos, insects, smuggling, and dirty fuel. Since you have to stop there for fuel, if you are going or coming from the Caribbean to the south, that thing about the dirty fuel is what they are most famous for.

Any captain that goes there regularly knows that a filter for the fuel you buy from their pump is an absolute essential. Experienced customers of this gas dock also maintain a close watch on the fuel gauge because the fuel sales manager has several storage tanks and it is normal for the supply to be switched more than once during refueling from one tank to another. The fuel comes to the gauge via very long pipes and each time they exchange the supply a generous helping of air rushes through the meter before fluid reaches it and all this is recorded as gallonage.

Considering that Inagua sells the most expensive fuel in the whole Commonwealth of The Bahamas (about twice the average cost at any given time in Florida), this business of selling air can be, and is, quite a good sideline.

Heading north, we went through the Crooked Island Passage with the tall white lighthouse on your right standing on Castle Island and the Mira Por Vos reef far over to the left. The water is very deep, almost to the beach there at Castle Island and it looks like a rainbow in all shades of blue as it comes up from three thousand feet to the bar which juts out from the point of the island. I never saw so many variations of blue anywhere else. I think it's because it is pure sand all the way to the depths and the water works like a pale filter and that unusual geography produces the bands of color.

It's a straight course all the way from Inagua to Clarence Town on Long Island, passing through the Crooked Island Passage. We got to the harbor in Clarence Town at about eight a.m. which is the absolutely best time to arrive. The sun is shining from behind you directly onto the gentle green hills that frame the postcard picture perfect town with two almost identical white churches with their twin conical spires. One pastor built both of them, and he must have had just the one construction plan and paint supplier.

He came there originally as an Anglican and built the first one then converted to the Catholic faith, became a priest, and built the second one. After a while, he figured that the place was a bit crowded—there must have been over a hundred people there at the time—and so he went over to Cat Island and built himself a hermitage on Comer Hill where the only thing he had to contend with was the odd sand fly or a passing land crab. His name was Pastor Jerome, Father Jerome, and then, finally, Hermit Jerome.

We spent three days at Clarence Town. They bake wonderful bread there without preservatives of any kind in the loaves. When you get it hot from the oven it feels like it would float away out of your hands. The next day it is a bit more solid, and, if you have been so foolish not to have eaten it by day three, you can either use it to drive nails, crack conch shells or throw it away and buy another one of the fresh loaves that they make daily.

There are a lot of crabs on this island, and the other food, besides the bread, which they are known for is crab and rice which is like shrimp and rice, only better. Conch is plentiful on the grass flats and they make an unforgettable conch stew after beating the conch meat with a mallet on flat stones. It's like a sort of conch jelly.

Long Island is a very interesting place with a strong, distinctive local culture. They grow crops in fissures blown out of the pure rock with small charges of dynamite. They fill these holes with compost and grow every type of tree and fruit bearing shrub. They call it pothole farming. I never met a Long Islander that was anything but friendly, courteous and helpful. As long as you are not in a hurry. That's not a virtue they appreciate —if it is a virtue.

There's a blind man there who owns a bar and he has a shirt with about a dozen pockets on the front. It's a cash register in disguise. When you buy a drink—or a bottle—he quotes you the price and then he asks you to tell him what money it is that you gave him. Let's say it is a twenty dollar bill. If the cost is five dollars and fifty cents he takes the correct bills and coins from the different pockets where those denominations are stored and gives you the correct change. He better stay in Long Island if that's how he expects people to conduct trade.

The last afternoon before we left I made some little bait pellets of bread and caught about twenty of the small-billed bait fish they call ballyhoo off the marina wharf with a very thin line and a tiny hook. Joyce asked me what they were for and I told her they would be very useful over the next week.

I was trying to save up little surprises for her. She

had never left her island home before and I wanted her to always remember this trip in a special way. I wasn't going to make another with her or anybody else, and I was being a little selfish in trying to make it my personal production. But it was more than that.

Coming out of Clarence Town harbor at ten in the morning the colors were as marvelous as ever with the dark blue, unmarked channel leading out and then trending to the north and the white sand banks on either side. As soon as you pass Strachan Cay you can lay a course close in along the island all the way north to Cape Santa Maria on the northern tip of Long Island with its miniature range of limestone cliffs and tiny lighthouse. Then you come around to a westerly heading and head for Galliot Cut. Once through that, you are in the shelter of the Exumas which is the most beautiful cruising ground in the whole Bahamas and that is saying something.

The whole chain stretches out before you all the way to Highbourne Cay which is only about thirty miles from Nassau. If you find one spectacular beach with a boat already anchored there and you don't feel like company—let's say you are a Hermit Jerome type—all you do is go a half mile, or less, further and you will have an equally perfect anchorage all to yourself.

There's one particular island there and on the shore there's a sign with an arrow on it that reads: "To the Spring." After a while, you will come to a few more of these notice boards as you ascend a footpath to the tree-shrouded summit of the cay where it also gets hotter with the climb in the baking sun. There you'll pass another sign reading: "You are Nearing the Spring." A few yards further, you come around a bend in the path and there's another that reads: "The Spring." This final sign is tied to a big rusty old coil spring that must have come from a truck. It is a simple kind of place and the humor is matched to the atmosphere.

I don't think there is a real spring with water in the whole of the Exumas so everybody likes to say they visited this one. They tell their friends who are planning a visit to the area about this island and tell them to make sure they go and have a look at this unique site. "Make sure you go and see the spring," they say. People who are unmoved by the sophisticated comic skill of Leno and Letterman will tell their friends to be certain to do this. It's difficult to explain. I guess it's too simple.

When you do pick a cay that is to your liking, you go in as close as you wish on the very gentle shelving edge of the Bahama Bank, which stands to the west of the islands, and stop in whatever depth you are comfortable with. In about ten minutes, at least one territorial barracuda that owns that piece of ground will swim up to see who has dropped in. This is when you float one of the ballyhoos back to him that you have brought from Long Island and he grabs it immediately and you have the barracuda for dinner.

They say some of the big ones carry the ciguatera poisoning, but I never heard of one having it in the Exumas. The barracuda for dinner was one of the little surprises I had for Joyce and she particularly appreciated it having come from a place where a meal of fresh fish was hard to catch anytime you wanted it.

They have so many cays in the chain that they don't all have names. There's even one officially called No Name Cay. You can't compare these cays. It would be a waste of time.

Taking eight days, we worked all the way up north to the group of islands named Allan's Group where they have a big population of iguana lizards. The last night there, we anchored very close to Leaf Cay which is a few yards from the biggest of the tiny Allan archipelago. That's where most of the iguanas live. I put out two bow anchors at right angles to each other because the current runs strongly past the island. Moored that way, you can relax when the tide shifts and you will swing in the opposite flow to that which prevailed just a few hours earlier in perfect safety.

It was a typical Bahama night with the east wind about eight or ten knots and a thousand million stars overhead and the shadowless light they make. The sandy salt smell breezed across the boat as it passed over the nearby island.

I was sitting up on the flying bridge and Joyce came over. Beautiful as ever. She asked me how I was feeling and I told her not bad. She asked me if there was something wrong and I decided to tell her. It was truly selfish, but I couldn't help it. There was still Nassau and Gun Cay left and then we would be in Miami, and I could have easily put it off until then, but I couldn't help it. So I told her.

I told her what I knew and what I had worked out by myself. I don't know why lots of doctors talk to you like you are a fool. I think they want to create the impression that you *are* a fool. This will make you hesitant to ask them what they plan to do about the problem and, then, if there is any honesty in them, they would probably have to say, "I don't have a clue." Which is embarrassing.

She sat on the little cushioned bench across the front of the bridge and listened and then she got up and came over to the helmsman's chair where I was and put her arms around me from behind. She said that before we had left she made a joke with one of her young friends that she would give me a heart attack in six months and go back to Jamaica as a wealthy widow and now she wished that she had never said anything like that, even in a joke. If I hadn't known it was her behind me, I would have hardly recognized her voice. She had absolutely no reason to tell me all of that, and she was crying when she said it. I never saw Joyce cry before.

After a while, I got up and we sat together on the bench seat. I had been with her for six years and married to her for just two weeks. She had been pure fun all the time and I never fooled myself about her. Really, I never did.

She stopped crying and we sat there. She put her head on my shoulder, which was a gesture quite out of character for her, and said, "I love you." She was a natural patois speaker and would have said, "Me love you," as a matter of course, but she used the formal *I* as if she was making a legal statement. She would say it again a few times afterward, but it was the first time she had ever said it. She was an honest girl, as far as I know.

That night we sat up there on the bridge and listened to the faint singing sounds that the iguanas make late at night. I never heard it anywhere else except at Leaf Cay in the Allan's.

Nassau was...well, Nassau is a tourist trap, but not a bad one. Joyce loved the huge aquarium they have at the Atlantis Hotel where you walk through a dimly lit tunnel, like a corridor, and the fish are beside you, and even above you, in the vast salt water enclosures with glass walls. There are groupers in there that would weigh over a hundred pounds. Jewfish they are, actually.

We went to one of the casinos on the Paradise Island side of New Providence and some security guard asked Joyce if she was a Bahamian and she answered him in an extra strong Jamaican accent with a few words that he must have only heard from angry Jamaicans. They have some rule about local people not being allowed to gamble there.

The penultimate leg of the trip from Jamaica to Florida takes you over the Silver Bank where the channel is called Larks Two Fathom Bridge. It has a minimum of twelve feet of clear water all across the shoal, but the water is so clear, and the sand so incredibly white, that it looks more like twelve inches.

On the day we crossed, there were dozens of schools containing anywhere from fifty to a hundred baby sharks in each group cruising all around over the smooth sea floor. The Silver Bank is a huge nursery for them.

On the west side, the shallow expanse ends with an irregular line of cays fencing the boundary to the Gulf Stream with Cat Cay and Bimini being the ones that offer the best place for a final stop to get the outward customs clearance when bound west for Miami. Bimini has never been quite able to throw off its preoccupation with being a big deal in the days of prohibition and is obsessed with trying to punch above its weight, so I prefer Cat Cay.

We spent our last night of the trip there. It is a thoroughly "American" marina and you know that you are basically finished with the Bahamas when you check in here, but at least Cat Cay is honest about it. We pulled out early in the morning for the final fifty mile voyage to the city of Miami. It's a city where lots of people go to prepare themselves to die.

Crossing the Gulf Stream here in the Straits of Florida, the northward flow is between two and three knots all the time. In a slower boat like mine, you set up a course roughly three miles south of where you want to end up for each hour that you figure the trip will take you. Nowadays, GPS takes all of that out of the picture, but I turned it off and dead reckoned it across like we did for all the years when I went back and forth regularly. It was an exercise in nostalgia.

When I saw the tall buildings behind the port of Miami come up right where they were supposed to, it was like the pleasure you get from solving a small puzzle. You can go right in on them until you see the breakwaters of Government Cut and then head in past Dodge Island with all the cruise ships lined up like giant ocean-going condominium blocks.

Over on the right is Watson Island where "Pappy" Chalk started his airline and used a beach umbrella to make an office. My father knew him. Old Pappy's airline kept a lot of thirsty people happy during prohibition and that's how the old man got to know him. My family has been in the contraband business from way back.

Well, I'm finished with all that and I'm not going anywhere again I guess.

I have the boat up for sale now and a broker is coming to show her this afternoon. One came yesterday, but I haven't gotten an offer yet. She's a bit slow, and the modern yachts are all at least five to ten knots or faster at cruising speed, but she's in good condition.

I rented a modest house on a canal that runs off Biscayne Bay, and I can see her tied up to the dock from the living room. I hope she gets a good owner. You get to feel personal about a boat—especially one that you used to live in. I okayed the brokers to take her out if the potential buyer insists on a sea trial. I don't go myself. I want the last time I was on her to be that voyage up here with Joyce. We sit in the living room and go over some of the events of our voyage together and that's another selfishness of mine, but she swears she likes to do it so I have decided to believe her. It was a wonderful trip.

The Desperate Cycle

CHAPTER 15

THE OFFICER IN COMMAND CONTEMPLATES A PROBLEM

The officer commanding the Coast Guard headquarters at Port Royal Base sat at his desk in the big, airy room with a wide view of the parade ground. From his window he could see his fleet of four ships. He anticipated being able to send one on a patrol as soon as the quartermaster could identify some money for fuel.

He was considering what on earth to do with Commander Singh. The man was infinitely more of a handicap than the chronic lack of funds. Commander Singh was an infernal problem. If only he had been a fool, there would have been no great difficulty. That would have made such a difference. But Mr. Singh was quite intelligent. A disaster as a person, and even more so as a uniformed representative of a service with a chief executive who detested bad publicity, but not stupid. Unfortunately.

The commanding officer had a nickname. His subordinates called him "Knock Softly." There seems to be more than one possible origin to this caption. Some said that it was better to knock softly on his door so as not to wake him. Others recommended the soft knock so that the commanding officer could ignore it and say later that he never knew there was a problem. This suited everyone and kept the base happy.

The commanding officer reflected on this loose cannon—Singh. If you put him along with regular police on secondment or military reconnaissance parties he was likely to do the most awful things. You could never nail them down, but they created rumors among certain sectors. Human rights groups and so on. If that was the extent of it, it would not be so bad, but there was much more serious stuff. Unforgivable behavior which had consequences. He might crack a few heads and it might have been better not to have done that, but it had little consequences. Not so if you committed serious breaches of protocol.

At some ceremony at the home of a big shot—the biggest shot, actually—of the coffee industry, Singh was reportedly conducting a most flagrant courting of that coffee baron's female personal assistant. The big man, or, to be more physically accurate, the very small big man, had intervened and Singh had apparently dismissed this miniature source of great influence and power as "stumpy."

Try as he might, the commanding officer had been unable to get a precise account of the event because the supposed insultee had refused to discuss the matter and Singh had said that he could not remember saying anything disrespectful.

Nonetheless, the bi-weekly arrival of a large box of the wonderful handpicked coffee, compliments of Mr. Akiyama, at the Coast Guard base had stopped abruptly. When the commanding officer had called personally to speak to Mr. Akiyama he had been addressed in a highly polite and exaggeratedly pleasant manner by the gentleman himself. Mr. Akiyama had said that the ravages of insects and inclement weather had so curtailed production that even small economies had been necessary on a temporary basis. The implication of Mr. Akiyama's remark was that a review of such cutbacks could be undertaken at any time should it appear pleasing to him. The commanding officer understood perfectly that Singh was not a pleasing presence to most people.

"It is so unfortunate," Mr. Akiyama had concluded the conversation. "Thank you for calling, sir. Please give me a ring anytime. Perhaps things will change soon. It might be very possible that change could come. Many things could change."

Now there was this other matter of the Custos of Portland. The first citizen in the parish. A title left over from colonial days, but a person—particularly in this case—of wealth and power who was also the owner of one of the most beautiful private yachts in the island.

In a most unfortunate accident, this yacht had drifted up on the beach at Bull Bay because of some series of incompetent errors by the crew delivering it back to its home port after a spell of shining, manicuring and polishing at the dry dock. Singh had been in command of a cutter returning from a cruise to the Morant Cays where he had been as unpleasant as usual to the poor fellows trying to scrounge a living around that series of open sandbars and fished-out reefs.

He had one of these unfortunates aboard the cutter right now for being in possession of four eggs of the wild terns which nested there. The four eggs were locked in a box marked "evidence" and placed in a small vault in the captain's cabin. The taking of these eggs was a breach of a wildlife protective act, but it was generally conceded by everyone—except Commander Singh—that these desperate residents of the cays could boil a few from time to time. Such leniency did not find room for inclusion in Commander Singh's strict personal manual of operations.

It so happened that the message concerning the stranding on the coast of the Custos' prize vessel had been passed to Singh who was in the immediate vicinity on his way back from the cays with his prisoner and the incriminating eggs. A few humorous remarks had circulated around the base that Singh ought to be sympathetic since it had not been so long ago when he had found himself in a similar grounding predicament when he had drifted up onto a mud bank with his embarrassingly disabled cutter. "What goes around..." seemed to be the general sentiment.

Commander Singh had approached the yacht where she was heeled very slightly over, resting in the almost flat calm on the hard coral sand where a very sharp decline to deep water would have facilitated a simple extraction. At this early stage, there would have been no significant damage. The bow was literally on dry land. This was enough for the legal mind of Singh.

He had noted in the log: "No danger to life and limb. Crew may leave the vessel at any time in perfect safety. Commercial salvage should be implemented to avoid appearance of interference in normal commercial operations by government agency." That log entry had been transmitted to the radio room at Port Royal, but not passed on to the commanding officer who was taking his regular mid-morning nap.

Well, that was awkward reasoning, but, strictly speaking, defensible. The problem was that the Custos had gotten hold of the cellular number for Mr. Singh around this time. Some said it was supplied by a brother officer who slipped it to the Custos after having heard the log entry. Perhaps he was certain that Singh would say something dreadful if the Custos called him. That detail of how the passing on of the number was done was never made clear.

In any case, the Custos had got Singh on the phone

and asked why assistance could not be rendered to the maritime apple of his eye, presently resting comfortably and, up to now, undamaged, on the sand, but which might be truly compromised if the sea breeze came in.

It was at this point that Commander Singh had justified the expectation of whoever had provided the mobile number. He had told the Custos that it was not the job of the officers and men and vessels of the Jamaica Defense Force, Coast Guard division, to remove flotsam and jetsam from the beaches of the island. That had been the end of the call. It was assumed that the Custos had been struck dumb at this description of his yacht. It had certainly made an impression on him.

Another catastrophe, thought the commanding officer. Three times a year this Custos had put on sumptuous banquets for the commanding officer and his chosen guests. Naturally, the commanding officer had never included Singh among his invitees, but they were occasions to which he, personally, looked with great anticipation. What an asshole that man Singh was!

The commanding officer thought of all opponents to his system of management in this term. He had acquired it from association with his many American trainers on various courses and used it as a badge of internationally obtained education. He had been a great admirer of Mr. Richard Nixon and had been most surprised that the United States seemed to have found that president at fault for some activities which had appeared to the commanding officer as perfectly appropriate. When he used the term "asshole," he felt that he was speaking in the style of his hero.

Something radical would have to be done to cut Singh down to size or, preferably, out of the picture entirely. Was it possible that the man needed some sort of counseling?

The commanding officer decided to consult the Army chaplain, who was a cheerful atheist with a good grasp of human nature. The chaplain had said that Singh had a messianic conviction. That was why, in his opinion, the normal, flexible backbone of a human being had been replaced in this specimen by a stainless steel rod. "Very well," the commanding officer had said, "but where does that lead us? What do I do about it?"

"Messiahs are often martyrs of some kind. Many of them desire crucifixion. Perhaps you could provide him with a cross and some nails?"

The commanding officer had thought long and hard about that. He knew that Singh harbored an almost fanatical fixation about the embarrassment visited upon him when miscreants had shackled together the propellers on his boat. He knew that Singh spent every spare hour digging into the background of the people believed to be responsible. The man was on the brink of irrationality over the incident.

The commanding officer thought that, given sufficient latitude, Singh could really disgrace himself on this matter to the point where he could be forced to resign "in the public interest." That would take care of him, especially if an operation could be so structured that the ramrod-spined commander would be completely responsible as the total architect of some gigantic failure. Nothing was certain, of course. But it was quite possible. Thus, the commanding officer decided to provide Mr. Singh with a suitable cross, a hammer of the correct dimensions, and a whole case of nails.

The Desperate Cycle

CHAPTER 16

THE COMMANDER TAKES COMMAND

In an office buried deeply within an anonymous building in the capital city of Kingston, six men sat down to discuss the task of "clearing up" what was becoming a developing problem.

For a long time, especially along the northeast and eastern end of the coast of the island, there had been a steady undercurrent of low level smuggling, some transshipment and original shipment of narcotics, and a trade in weapons exchanged for marijuana, which was very intermittent and, consequently, the hardest nut to crack. The latter was often associated with approaching elections when rival party enforcers made preparations to provide the proper level of encouragement to those whose political loyalty might be wavering. This encouragement was modeled on the Latin American gangster doctrine of offering payment in either silver or lead.

At one time, the commissioner of police had removed and replaced the entire complement of a whole station having apparently come to the conclusion that the complete division was implicated. The effect had been very short term. Anecdotal evidence was abundant but hard facts elusive. There was so much homegrown accommodation for the trade, particularly the drug trade, mixed in with the fear that somehow high officials with power were involved, that an effective campaign to enroll civilian cooperation had stalled for years. Recently, the stall had become a general retreat.

The other enormous problem was that the money which seeped into the civilian population from these unofficial activities generated an almost benevolent local attitude. This prevailed even among people not directly connected to outright illegality.

Thus, the feeling developed that, although unfortunate, the inescapable fact was that the whole thing was "good for the economy." Once that enters the equation, it can become the greatest obstacle to making any significant inroads in the fight to enforce the rule of law. The position becomes entrenched along these lines: "What do you have to offer us that is going to replace what is going on? You want me starve and cut sugar cane? You want us to fish over dead bottom? You have anything better for us to do?"

But there was an opportunity emerging in the specific location which Commander Singh now regarded as a proving point at which to assert law and order, not to mention obtain revenge for his impaired dignity.

The type of gang warfare that had turned parts of Kingston and, to a lesser extent, Montego Bay into violent enclaves, armed to the teeth and virtually conceded to miniature warlords, had not become a widespread phenomenon of life in rural Jamaica or even in the much larger parish capitals.

But the appearance of incidents heralding the approach of what is generally called "gang warfare" was emerging as a feature of life in the town where Commander Singh had recently suffered some discomfiture when his vessel was stranded in the mud. Even at his own base, there had been some subdued hilarity at the idea of the immaculate commander's involvement in anything quite so grimy as the soft harbor sludge. Awareness of this was never far from Singh's consciousness, but he restrained himself. He proceeded cautiously and in accordance with his own internal logic and discipline.

Commander Singh had used every contact he could muster to convene this meeting. It comprised staff at a very high level of the three branches of the security forces. Naturally, it was carefully kept one notch below the absolute top echelon so that deniability, as well as a slightly greater flexibility in methodology, was possible. He had been slightly surprised at how easy it had been to arrange this summit. Even his half-dead fool of a commanding officer had been genuinely helpful—even encouraging—for a change.

Commander Singh's message was simple: "We have an opportunity to break the back of this situation if we act now. And at this place!" Singh stabbed his finger at the map with uncharacteristic real emotion. That is how it must be sold. A line in the sand! The competition between criminal elements here—right here—was inhibiting the ability of the local gangs to function.

Now, in their moment of weakness, is the time to

confront and destroy them. Of equal importance, the local perception that these skirmishes might balloon into truly deadly proportions was spreading. The fear was building that these "wars" were likely to engulf the whole town. This would give a golden opportunity to gain acceptance for measures that the public at large might otherwise meet with stubborn resentment. Inconveniences, curtailment of some degree of civil liberties, and even collateral damage became acceptable to ordinary citizens under certain extreme circumstances. But we cannot waste time. As they say, "never waste a crisis." Now is the moment. Thus, he presented the case.

And he had fairly accurate inside information on the chosen place. He had made useful contacts there and had a few men on the ground. He had names, not just rumors. He had profiles that showed patterns of behavior and therefore vulnerability in known criminals. Commander Singh was disarmingly forthcoming.

"I have no intention of forgetting about anything down there. A tactical retreat is just a maneuver." He paused, then went on. "I can tell you something else. This whole project has to be run from outside. Only the minimal formal courtesy must be extended to the local cops. I would not trust one of them from the top down. They are either incompetent or corrupt and sometimes both. In any case, they are useless or worse than useless. Just get the divisional chief to explain to them that their job is to keep out of the way." That last bit sounded very much like an order to the senior police superintendent across the table. Nothing happened, so he felt reassured.

He was gradually asserting his position as potential coordinator of the task force. He had already very carefully handpicked a few men and one woman from his own branch of service and was ready to go. The upsurge of destabilizing violence was all he had been waiting for. Once that starts it won't be long before an extra dead body or two on the street becomes commonplace. Nothing special.

He knew it was going to be okay when the Member of Parliament for the district called him personally to congratulate him on what the MP called, guardedly, "The Initiative." It was understood that a joint military, police and Coast Guard enterprise was going to be launched to restore peace and tranquility to his constituency. He recognized that at this stage a certain level of confidentiality should be maintained.

Later, when complete success had been achieved, he would have a press conference and expected the commander to remember that invaluable support from the political representative had been there with them from the start.

The commander did not believe for a second that anything more than hot air was obtainable from this source or that the population in general would be so gullible as to believe it either. His opinion had been reflected in a piece of graffiti that he had observed recently on a white wall along a street which ran through a notoriously crime-ridden slum. Trying to stimulate support for an upcoming by-election, an ardent activist of one of the participants had painted one morning a message of hope and expectation designed to resonate with the voters:

CANDIDATE JOHNSON TO THE RESCUE!

By afternoon, a skeptic had written below:

OF THE GUNMEN.

That, Commander Singh believed, was the overall truth as it existed in the popular culture and was backed up by his own life experience. He functioned within his personal philosophy and there were still a few others who shared his convictions among his service. He did not deal in degrees of dedication.

There was always the possibility that some of these others, even within his own circle of associates, did not hold his pure intentions with the same intensity. He always had to be prepared to contend with that. It was the most difficult element to assess perfectly. He hoped that he would not have to encounter it during what was coming, or, should that arise, that it would not do so at a particularly crucial moment.

This element of weakness in human nature, which halted otherwise committed colleagues, had produced unpredictable hesitation in situations of crisis. He had worked on eradicating any residues of it in his own character and was supremely confident that he had been successful. He proceeded with the certainty of a man on a mission. Singh the missionary. Coming to the rescue. No postscript would ever be required to qualify which side he was on. He was on the side of the angels.

One week into the Singh-led operation—codenamed "Crack Down"—it began to look to Jinks like things were not going to be as difficult as he had feared. A few of his very lowest ranked followers had been taken in for "processing" and all were back on the street. The term processing had no real basis in the legal system. It involved a sweep by joint police/military forces of a street corner, or other gathering spot, and the wholesale scooping up of all young men and often a few young women.

These "suspects" were taken to a holding area and "processed," which was a vague term. It might mean a few hours of discomfort and humiliation or it might mean being crammed into a stifling-hot, unventilated cell for days and nights until a few actually died. That had actually happened in a jail at the Constant Spring lockup some years previously. Another paroxysm for Amnesty International to bleat about, provoking a local senior policeman to refer to the members of that, and local allied organizations, as the "human wrongs people." Commander Singh had appropriated the phrase but refrained from using it in public utterances.

Among the adherents of the two other rival gangs— or posses as they preferred to be called—quite unequal experiences were occurring and the word was spreading. These unfortunate anti-Jinks forces disappeared into the maw of detention and most were transferred to Kingston to face charges the existence of which they had previously been unaware. A small quantity of relatively lucky ones was released and came back with the impression that they had received especially severe treatment. Were these to be regarded as "messengers?"

The rumor began to circulate that Jinks was somehow "connected" and a huge resentment began to develop in the harsh little underworld. An assumption of official protection in their environment invited the likelihood that this immunity could only come from being an informer. That was about the worst label that could be hung around your neck. Jinks warned everyone that the danger from unofficial elements was almost certainly greater than that presented by the numerous new patrols and very frequent, and apparently random, road blocks.

These "spot checks," as they were called, took no notice of, or made even a pretense of abiding by, the doctrine defined as probable cause. It was understood that they were designed to *Break the Back of the Monster of Crime* as the newspaper described it. Civilians had to put up with the inconvenience of suddenly finding a major roadway blockaded while every vehicle had its documents meticulously scrutinized, its trunk inspected and a small interrogation carried out on the driver and, sometimes, the passengers.

The nature of these interviews largely depended on the appearance of the people in the car. If they looked like they had taken a bath within the last twenty-four hours and spoke Standard English it was carried out in a far more genteel manner than when the occupant or occupants of the automobile—and particularly truck or bus—clearly belonged to the abusable class. This is presumably one of the deadly legacies of slavery. As psychiatrists tell us: The abused child often becomes the abuser.

The Desperate Cycle

CHAPTER 17

THE END OF A CYCLE

Sunday morning. Very light traffic. Even lighter than usual for a Sunday. A sudden mid-morning squall had blown in from the sea and spoiled some people's plans for a swim.

After the flurries of rain passed, the wind that had brought the sudden downpour ashore picked up considerably, blowing away the last traces of moisture and flecking the ocean with whitecaps as far out as the eye could see. It was rapidly driving the last vestiges of the clouds inland to pile them up on the blue peaks where Mr. Akiyama's coffee grew.

When the little open-backed van passed by, the police officers, who had been standing on the wide grassy verge of the road leading out into the high country above the town, closed the check point. They parked a motorcycle in the middle of the road. One of them spoke into a handheld radio.

Half a mile further along the road there was a deep bend and then a short, straight stretch. On the left side, there was a narrow strip of flat "shoulder," then the land fell away sharply all the way down to where the sea was piling up, sending plumes of spray skyward as it pounded on the rocky coast.

On this piece of level grassy ground, a black car with tinted windows was parked. The bonnet was open and fixed in the upright position by its stay-rod. A woman dressed in a pretty yellow morning outfit stood beside the car looking properly distressed. The heavy breeze pressed her light clothes against her body.

Sprinter stopped his van just in front of this scene and got out. He was not an expert at this sort of thing, but any man who runs a boat with a single engine has learned some of the basics. If he could not get the car started that might be even better. That might involve giving the stranded lady a lift and who knows where that might lead. Just look at the job the wind was doing.

We are on the side of the angels and, look, even God's elements assist us!

Sprinter walked toward the car. The woman stepped back onto the edge of the road. The back door on the far side opened and a tall man got out. He leveled a pistol across the roof of the car and shot Sprinter once. When Sprinter fell, he did so only as far as his knees, so the man aimed carefully and shot him a second time, hitting him where he could be absolutely certain that it would be the last one required.

The rushing air had whipped away the sound of the two explosions, but they had been loud enough. Loud enough to wake somebody.

The tall man began walking the few steps to where Sprinter lay. *Just checking, angels.* That was when both the tall man and the woman saw the other door of Sprinter's van opening. A little boy got out, rubbing his eyes. He looked confused. But, pretty soon, he headed straight for the man on the ground. He knelt beside the quiet form. "Get up, Daddy," he said. Even with the sweeping wind pulling the words away, you could hear what he said quite clearly. He said it more than once and he said it louder each time.

The tall man hesitated for a moment. But just for a moment. He raised his arm. The pistol was still in his hand. The woman stepped directly in front of him. "No," she said. "You are my superior officer, but you can't do that. You'll have to kill me before you do that. How you figure to explain that? I understand the other business, but you can't do that. I say you can't do it."

A radio clipped to the tall man's belt crackled out a very brief message. He missed the content of the message with the noise of the wind and he took it and held it up to his ear. He went back, grimfaced, to the car and got in the front passenger side.

The woman got in and drove off the road and up an unpaved, decaying farm access-way. It led in a big circle and then back to the mountain road a few miles further on. When they got back to the main highway, there was almost no traffic coming out of the town. Most vehicles had stopped at the amazing scene further back and a considerable crowd was forming.

No police cars or other officials arrived for some time. The first one that got there told the crowd to get back and out of the way so that they could begin collecting evidence. They told the spectators, "We need to take proper care to obtain all the clues here so as to 'break the back of the monster of crime'. This is what happens when criminals start fighting it out. Not even the highways are safe." That sounded very reasonable to everyone.

By early that afternoon, Jinks' gang was effectively destroyed. Among the hierarchy, only Rocky escaped and that was because he was trying to find a place to hide Lucy and Peter and was not in the gang's blockaded lane when an overwhelming force of heavily armed police bottled up Jinks and his associates. They took Jinks and four of his chief lieutenants away in a jeep and the report said that, on the way to the jail, these desperate outlaws tried to pull concealed weapons and stage an escape and were killed in a "shootout."

All five—later to be called "The Gang of Five"— were taken to the hospital and pronounced dead on arrival. A quite unbelievable story began to circulate that when the jeep arrived at the medical facility a porter noticed that one of the bodies was still trying to lift its head. It was rumored that this was pointed out to the driver who said he would be right back.

The jeep, so went the totally impossible yarn, drove

away and returned a few minutes later at which time no further movement was observable. No law-abiding citizen gave any credence to this fantasy which was clearly a fabrication made up by mischievous elements. And suppose it was true. Of course it isn't, but just suppose. No omelets are made without breaking some eggs. Got to break the back of the monster of crime.

Rocky chartered a taxi and took Lucy and the still bewildered little boy with him. He convinced Lucy that it would only be a matter of time before, at the very least, Peter would have some sort of accident. Rocky had talked for a long time with the child and it was clear that he had seen quite enough. Far too much.

As soon as it got dark, they drove to the big gates of the old sewage treatment plant. Rocky told the driver to park beyond the entrance. There were plenty of places in the old uncared for fence where anyone could enter below the big crumbling signs that state: "No Trespassing."

One small light showed where the caretaker would be watching or sleeping or doing whatever he felt like as was the undisputed right of the monarch of even a very diminutive kingdom of ancient effluent. Rocky stood outside the large concrete building which had once been the office block and called out, "Mr. Barton."

He tried it softly at first, out of natural caution, then, realizing there were deserted scrub and overgrown paving stretching for at least two hundred yards between the street and where Mr. Barton presumably was roosting, he repeated it louder. The caretaker was not a young man. It was quite likely that only relatively high volume speech might penetrate his consciousness.

The Desperate Cycle

CHAPTER 18

MR. BARTON'S EMPIRE

The musings of Mr. Aston Barton, ex-trainee manager, overseer of ex-tertiary sewage plant No. 1, retired overseer, caretaker/janitor, premises now unspecified, unofficial landlord. Nature lover. Specialist in invisibility. Lord of all he now surveys.

The first year was the trickiest. I had the job as watchman, but no person with the final authority wanted to officially mothball the disused plant. It had become politically toxic as well as genuinely so. Remember, it had been a showcase project once and there were plenty of people around who remembered that and even some who recalled the enormous loans and guarantees that the government had assumed during the construction. Those loans were still a burden on the taxpayer.

When it was finally downgraded to a straight pass-through system, with the inflowing liquid and what went into the sea being identical, a campaign to render the whole facility invisible began.

You think a huge sewage processing depot can't vanish? It's perfectly possible and, as we know, "politics is the art of the possible," as the Old Prussian said. Just give them time.

The problem was that for a while there was no alternative, so, every now and then, a visiting tour of the least dreadfully decayed sections would be arranged on the basis that a renovation was still pending to be determined by the outcome of various feasibility studies. Expensive feasibility studies. So I had to be careful. Officially, I was just there at night. There were still a couple of old timers sitting around waiting to be pensioned off. They used to sit and play cards and dominoes with me all day.

Eventually, the last of the daytime staff went and I got moved up a rung to caretaker. That was when they finally diverted most of the big intakes and only a few "greywater" drains fed through here. I was to report any obvious blockage that might occur, but I never had to do that.

I had known the plant so well that I could shunt the waste water around or just let it overflow. It all went to the same place no matter what you did now that all the treatment tanks were out of the picture. So what the hell difference did it make how it got there? They never heard from me and I joined the plant in a state of semi-invisibility. That's when they really forgot about me and the whole facility. I still got the pension and the little payment as caretaker.

Nobody ever came here anymore so I relocated into what had been my office and fixed it up quite nice. I took the windows that still had glass in them from other offices and put them in my "flat." I got myself a big desk by cutting the old boardroom table in half. I can tell you I had it better than most government pensioners. A home with lots of land and a view of the sea.

I also learned to mind my own business. Various sorts of human rejects drifted through the compound, scrapping it as they went. A few derelicts of doubtful sanity slept here and there between the tanks or inside the remains of the pumping stations. The people who lived in the ghetto across the highway all knew me, and I never felt threatened although there were some very tough types around. If you're a fixture, they usually leave you alone. Another degree of invisibility.

The night this fellow, Rocky, brought a young woman and a little boy and asked me to give them shelter because "they were in great danger," I didn't like it one bit. The last thing I wanted was anything dangerous. He told me that they would be under the protection of someone and when he told me who it was I felt a little better. The name he gave me was a very big, very dangerous person himself.

How was I to know if that was really the case? Rocky said that he would bring one of the close associates of this senior don to see me in the morning to prove it. Seems Rocky knew him through a mutual friend named Jinks from another part of town and he had cleared it with the big man himself. Turned out to be true.

The woman and the kid never gave me any trouble. She got a visit every week or two from this Rocky, and he must have brought some money. She used to ask me to buy a few things for her and the child. She never went out. I fixed up another office for them. Sometimes Rocky gave me a little cash. That's always welcome. It was my first experience as a landlord.

One time, Rocky asked me to show him some of the place and I took him on a tour. Showed him a little of how the operation had functioned. The big pumps and settlement beds and the water storage tanks with the last of the pelicans still perched on the rims. Nowadays, there were a lot of black turkey vultures—what we call "John Crows"—with their bare heads sharing space with the pelicans.

By now I figured out that Rocky must have joined up with the big man who had offered the protection and must be a sort of gangster himself. He began to look more and more the part as time passed. He was a tough-looking fellow. Not particularly tall, but very strong looking. He never roughed me up in any way, though.

When he would come he spent a lot of time with the kid. Seems the kid's old man had been knocked off by someone and the kid had seen it. Rocky would go over it quietly and patiently with the boy like he was trying to make very, very sure about the details and the description of who killed his father. He did it about twenty times to my knowledge and the mother told me she didn't like it, but for the moment Rocky had her scared to death that the murderer was going to eliminate the child, and maybe her too as witnesses, so she put up with it. She didn't seem to think she had a lot of choices. Maybe she never did have a lot of choices. Like so many of us.

They had been with me nearly a year when Rocky came by late one night. He stopped on the street. He had always come by himself before, but this time he had another fellow with him that looked like a barely controlled maniac. This one gave me the creeps.

Rocky came down to where I lived. He asked me to open the big gate. That was a formidable job in itself. The hinges were rusted and frozen all to hell. It took the three of us to push one of the sides far enough back that the car they had could drive through. It was pitch dark up by the gates except for the lights of the car, so I left the gate partly open figuring no passer-by would notice. Or care.

After they were in the open yard, they shut off their headlights and gave me a flashlight. Rocky said for me to walk ahead and guide them so they could drive the car to where the biggest of the old tanks were. There had been paved roads leading to all these operational areas once, but only patches of the asphalt remained with deep ruts and potholes and even tiny trees between. We had to go very slowly. Rats dashed away from us as we made our way to what had been called the "tank farm" in the old days.

Rocky parked the car as close as he could to the side of the twenty-foot high concrete wall of the most massive tank. He and the wild-looking, glittery-eyed one took four packages out of the trunk of the car. Each was wrapped tightly in plastic garbage bag type material with duct tape around it.

The iron spiral staircase that went to the top catwalk was shaky, but Rocky had gone right up it the time I had shown him around. He knew that it was still usable.

They had to make two trips each. Each parcel was quite big and they needed one hand to hold the rail. I held the flashlight and followed them with the beam to help with visibility.

When they had dropped the last one into the bottom of the old tank, which was cracked all over, but still held a few feet of rain water from time to time, they sat on the bonnet of the car and smoked a joint each. They were young guys, but heavy smokers so they were out of breath. The crazy one looked worse than ever.

I told them to call me to help with the gate when they were ready to get going. Rocky said okay. He said they would be off in a few minutes, and were just finishing their smokes. I started to head toward the gate. Everybody thinks I must be a bit deaf at my age and I like it that way. As a general rule, it's nice to hear more than people think you do. Not always. But it often is.

I was only about twenty feet away when I heard Rocky say to his partner, "What you think, Willie? He fit nice into those bags...for such a tall son of a bitch." I went on out of range quicker. I didn't want to hear any more of it.

About a week later, the woman, whose name I had discovered was Lucy, came and told me that she and the boy would be leaving. She said that Rocky had promised her that the threat to them had somehow become a thing of the past. Time must have taken care of it. That's what she said.

I was getting used to having them around, and the novelty of being a sort of landlord, but I could hardly expect that she would want to live here forever and raise her kid in an abandoned sewage farm. She said a lady friend of Rocky's named Joyce had just come back to the island after inheriting some money. Seems this Joyce's husband had keeled over suddenly.

This friend was going to open some little seaside hotel and restaurant back where they came from on the outskirts of the town and, as a favor to Rocky, was going to give her a job there and a place to live. It would mean she could put the boy Peter back in school. It sounded like things were working out for them.

I hoped the kid would cheer up. He always looked slightly out of it and spent hours on end staring out to sea. He had a disconnected style. He never really showed much interest in anything. Of course, a ruined and abandoned waste-water plant was not exactly Disney World, but I have seen young boys entertain themselves successfully with matchboxes sailing in a gutter. I had lots of watery gutters and bits of wood around this place, but not even that boyhood activity seemed to suggest itself to him. I hoped school would interest him.

When Rocky came for Lucy and Peter, I took him aside and asked him to do me a special favor. I asked him not to come back with that glassy-eyed inhuman freak and throw any more stuff in the old tank. I said, "Can I ask you that? As a personal favor?" And he said that was fine. That it had been a special occasion. Then he said, "You is not so deaf, are you, Mr. Barton?" And I said, "Oh, yes, I am, Rocky. But I can smell good." That seemed to satisfy him.

A while later, I heard that the lunatic cokehead one —the weirdo Rocky had called Willie—got held on some charge and died in prison. The story was that he hanged himself. Could be true. I suppose after he told them what they wanted to know he might as well have done that.

A few days after that took place there was an official report stating that Robert "Rocky" Brown had been accosted by a police party, suddenly pulled a gun, and was killed in the subsequent shootout. Perfectly understandable. Happens all the time. Here today, gone tomorrow.

Everything is just about back to normal around here. It almost seems as though there is some slight improvement taking place in the harbor. It's funny how you get to notice little changes even though they take place very slowly.

First of all, it's been a long time since we had any oil spill and, although I guess there must be a fair amount of it down at the bottom, it's been a few years since I could smell it so maybe it is getting absorbed or sinking or covered up or something. If you give the sea just the ghost of a chance it tries to recover.

They have a new treatment plant working at the other end of the bay and it is supposed to be handling about thirty percent of the sewage. I think the Chinese built it and everybody seems to agree that we ought to be able to pay for it in a century or two. I guess I've reached an age and stage when I find it hard to be blinded by a silver lining.

Not completely though.

I can still see them. And last month I saw one—a marvelous thing. Well, it was marvelous to me. A pelican started building a nest in one of the old almond trees. I didn't think I would ever live to see that again.

There mightn't be any future for the fellow in the bag or the two guys who dropped him in the tank, but if there was a future for the pelicans, I would settle for that.

If only we don't have any more oil spills, who knows what might happen.

The Desperate Cycle

CHAPTER 19

ON THE HOLDING OF A PERSON'S INTEREST

Lucy, Peter and the head teacher at Peter's school were having another of their many afternoon meetings. The head teacher was a weary-looking lady who wore little round spectacles covered in scratches. She looked at you with her head tilted back, trying to see better through the clearer glass below where the scratches dominated. She was graying at forty.

"He really is just not interested in anything," the head teacher said to Lucy. "That's the problem. He likes to play pranks sometimes and he will spend time and energy planning that. Like the time he tied Mrs. Weston's car to a tree so neatly, and concealed the rope so well, that nobody noticed. Poor Mrs. Weston. She has never mastered the art of engaging the clutch smoothly and has the most unfair nickname of Mrs. Bullfrog because she always progressed, as a driver, in a series of small leaps.

"When Peter had been identified as the culprit in the anchoring of Mrs. Weston's car, he had said that he wanted to see what would happen when she took off. That was what he said! I, personally, asked him where he had got the idea and he said that his 'Uncle' Rocky had told him a story once about how his father had tied up a boat and became famous for doing it.

"Then there was the time he connected a very long piece of fishing line all the way from the school bell actuator and had it sound for the end of the day fifteen minutes before time. Both those 'jokes', as he calls them, were quite clever in their way although very, very wrong, of course. But as far as his work is concerned, we have tried everything and he just drifts along. He will soon be thirteen and he is a very big boy physically, as you know, but he is going nowhere. Nowhere at all."

Lucy nodded. They had been over this familiar ground several times. She did not expect to get anywhere on this occasion either, but she was going through the motions. She had the impression that the head teacher was doing the same.

On the head teacher's desk was a file with Peter's name on it. *She must be just keeping it up to date*, Lucy thought. The two women looked at each other—sisters in a world of prolonged, although never quite accepted, defeat. Lucy saw blurred, grazed glasses and the head teacher saw Lucy's eyes which were twenty years older than the face which held them. A Jamaican mother's face.

Peter was sitting slightly apart from the head teacher and his mother as if to emphasize that all this had little to do with him. He was looking out through the big window at the wide blue sea. A big powerboat was heading to the west, leaving a long white wake behind as the powerful engines pushed the vessel through the ocean at thirty knots.

He was waiting as patiently as he could manage to get out of here and down to the beach which fronted the little guest house where he and his mother lived and where his mother was employed. Just last month he had finally finished months of work on a little abandoned skiff that had drifted ashore.

He had spent hundreds of hours begging for screws, pieces of wood and leftover tins with a little paint in them. Every tradesman on the construction sites within walking distance of his home had come to know Peter and his project. They would collect pieces of off-cut board, a few nails and screws and a half pot of glue and save them for him. Sometimes he would take a piece of wood to one of the carpenters and the man would cut and plane it along the marks which Peter had made.

He did not bring this up when the head teacher had said that he was not interested in anything. He made no intervention in the formal exchanges taking place between the head teacher and his mother. The conversation bored him. It would be too difficult to explain.

He made no effort to describe his intense interest in his grandfather's preserved pails of fishing tackle which had remained all these years stored in an abandoned old gear house. Every line on the aged wooden reels, traces, leaders and sinkers was now arranged in perfect order with the chafed or otherwise damaged parts cut off. Each one of the rust-blunted hooks had been removed and discarded. New sharp ones from the cases that the old man had left, packed in oiled boxes, had been retied and linked back to the main cord.

He had been very interested in doing that. Even the old bottle lamp stands were restored. He had cut the whole bottom off the cast net. The rope at the base was rotten, but the lead weights were impervious to salt water and time. Anyway, it had been a bit too long for him and now, in its shorter resurrected size, suited him better. One morning, he saw a mosquito net dumped in a garbage container and he made a new push net from it.

The first day he rowed the little boat out from the beach, he had not told anybody. He liked doing things on his own. In his own way. He spent that afternoon exploring. He found a deep break in the reef near the channel where the rocks opened for a short space, then came back up for a few more yards, then finally falling away to form the mouth of the main entrance of the ships channel.

Everybody said there were no fish left around, but he discovered that was not quite true. He found small schools of reef snapper, grunts and green jacks in this little pocket. He went on along the reef, studying it minutely, discovering several other tiny breaks and that each held small colonies of life. It was very calm, so he ventured beyond the reef a small distance and found spurs where the uneven profile of the natural barrier possessed crooked finger-like extensions probing out into the deeper water.

His next project would be to build a bottom viewer using a square piece of window glass and four bits of wood encasing the pane. It would be necessary to seal the glass to the wood perfectly, but he had sealed a whole boat bottom successfully so that could hardly be too much trouble.

The bottom viewer would allow him to see into the places where depth blurred perception from the surface. He had not even brought a line with him on this, his first voyage in the little skiff. He was learning at this stage. Attending one of the most ancient schools where man has studied. He could not imagine being bored along the reef.

He started fishing in these small, ignored spots and every time he got back he would have a few pounds of fish that Joyce, who owned the guest house, took from him and gave him some money in exchange.

He felt comfortable being around Joyce. That was not something he felt in the company of most people. She was a little on the chubby side, full of laughter and always hugging him and telling him to hurry and grow up. She would always joke, "Another year or so and you and me will be even better friends. That's a little secret joke, Pete. Just between you and me." He enjoyed that joke and he was interested in it. He particularly liked the privacy of the promise.

The first time he told his mother he was going to go night fishing she tried to talk him out of it, but it was not a very powerfully stated objection. She was quietly pleased that at last he seemed to be showing real enthusiasm for something. But it was necessary to raise concern at the night expedition. Just the normal amount that she would have been expected to make thereby hopefully alerting him to be especially careful and not go into the channel, or even cross it, because a big ship would never see his little bottle lamp and could run over him. He understood that long before she brought it up.

Many times in the day he had observed the passage of the big ocean-going container vessels and tankers as they approached the port and sometimes had been forced to pull hard on one side of the oars to bring the skiff to an angle where their sharp-peaked wakes would pass safely underneath. He knew the sort of power they contained. He had heard it clearly a hundred yards away in the beat of the monster engines.

He loved to watch them outbound as they cleared the last of the markers, which was called the farewell buoy, and began to feed the extra fuel to the engines and the bow wave blossomed white as they reached their cruising speed. He loved them and respected them and instinctively understood the image of release they brought to him as they shook off the confines of the harbor and gained the freedom of the open sea.

That afternoon, he begged the old Chinese man who owned the grocery store for a box of squid. Everybody called this man Mr. Chin although his name was Wong-Chu-On. Every Chinese man in Jamaica is Mr. Chin unless he insists otherwise. Mr. Chin said he could have one on credit, but the first ten pounds of fish was to come to him in payment for the bait. Peter, who up to now had never brought ten pounds of fish back from any trip, promised Mr. Chin that he would give him the first twelve pounds.

Peter got to the tip of the reef just as it was getting dark. He began his set so close to the point where the reef broke away that he was over the part where the bottom was just shifting from hard rock to the soft mud of the channel bed. So carefully had Peter studied this shelf that he could lay the whole length of the line precisely along where this changing terrain ran parallel to the bank where the eastern sequence of markers flashed green for entering vessels to follow, ensuring that they were in safe water.

He had fished it in the day and it was always a little better than most other places, but he knew, with the certainty and optimism of the young researcher, that the night would be much better. It had been years since anyone had bothered to fish inside the harbor at all. He planned to tend the line all night. The idea of sleep, which overcame him so readily in the weekday classroom, never once occurred to him here.

With the whole expanse of the night and his work stretched out before him, he felt as though he needed nothing more than that.

In the gray light of the morning, he began taking in the line finally after combing along it four times for the night. As each leader came aboard, he pinned it to the rim of one of the pails so that the whole assembly was neatly arranged and ready for the next time. In the box at the stern of the skiff were more than fifty red snappers of sizes ranging from a quarter of a pound in weight up to four fine specimens that would go a bit over two pounds each. They had always been the fish of the late night. Still, no catch on a scale to compare with his grandfather's youth, but explainable only by the fact that they had been neglected for a long time and the ocean and her children are so hard to kill.

On the last set, with the dawn just beginning to streak the sky, he had caught other types of fish, too. Three drummers and a sennett which is a small relative of the barracuda. These were all species that he had never taken before in his short career. Peter the record breaker!

Just as he was retrieving the last fifty feet of line, he felt the overboard part stiffen and then come very tight. He held it firmly, lest the hooks from behind start to slip back, and knew that it was not something dangerous.

One afternoon, he had hooked a small yellowtail snapper and a shark had appeared from nowhere and swallowed the fish before he could bring it in. The shark had swum away without apparently even being aware that he was, technically speaking, hooked and Peter had felt the supreme confidence and disdain of the shark in his immunity to the insignificant resistance that Peter presented. That had been an impressive lesson in superior power reminiscent of the ocean-going ships.

But this was quite different. This was a fish which knew that it was at a real disadvantage and was contesting the issue as vigorously as possible. A wonderful fish, nonetheless.

When he had got past the intervening leaders, and the problem presented by the necessity of evading the hooks on them, Peter impaled the fish with the gaff he had made months ago, but never had the necessity to use prior to this great occasion. It was a big pompano that would weigh close to ten pounds. When Peter had it aboard, he looked at the silver and blue streaks on his prize. They would only be visible for a few minutes before they faded as the pure oxygen invaded the bloodstream of the fish. Then he looked at the now-brilliant daybreak sky and knew a happiness that was unequaled in his life.

At that moment, he was sure that he had been born to be a fisherman. Everybody said that was a waste of time, but he would surely try. He hoped he would be able to do it. People said that something better than that would come along. Even Joyce said so. But, secretly, he hoped it would not.

He guessed he had thirty or forty pounds in the box plus the big pompano. He supposed that Joyce would take whatever was left after he discharged his debt to Mr. Chin, but he thought that he would test the wider commercial market now that he considered himself a graduate from the ranks of the amateurs. He had never sold a fish to anyone except Joyce and had no scale, but he rowed toward the marina where he knew foreign yachts moored. He was aware that visitors had money and spent it on a quite different basis to local people. They seemed to buy items on the basis of simply wanting them. This was a strange concept in the world in which Peter lived.

The ancient watchman saw him come in to the T-head. He came down to where Peter had stopped and said, "You can't land here, boy."

Peter told him he only wished to see if anybody wanted a really fresh snapper or two. The old watchman peered over the edge and looked in the box. He was suitably impressed. He had thought that a catch of that size was a thing of the past. A young white man with jet black hair combed back and tied in a tiny ponytail had come out of one of the big powerboats that were tied up to a finger pier. The man said, "Good morning, Mr. Miller. Have we received a visitor?" He had a strong Spanish accent.

"This boy have some fish he just catch this morning," said the watchman. "You want any, Mr. Martinez?"

The young man asked Peter to row around to where his boat was. It was too high to conduct any transaction from the crest of the big dock to the level of Peter's little skiff. Peter came alongside and the young man gave him a line to tie up beside the beautiful Viking motor yacht which was apparently his.

He wanted to buy the whole catch, but Peter knew the future value of Mr. Chin. The Chinese were all known to be shrewd investors rather than gullible pushovers. He particularly felt the need to show Joyce some of what he had caught. He intended that Joyce should see how he was already growing up fast in the fishing department and that this might shave some time off the probationary period she had decreed concerning her secret promise.

So he said that, unfortunately, he could only sell about ten pounds or so. He expressed his sorrow that he could not sell more but intimated that, as a professional, he had his regular customers and would not wish to disappoint them. He had no scale. This was purely because he had forgotten to bring one of several which he owned with him. Must have left it in one of the larger boats which he normally used. But he would guess the weight and be generous. The young man smiled and said that would be fine and selected two snappers and the big pompano and gave Peter more cash than he could remember ever having possessed at any one time.

This morning was producing all sorts of new intriguing experiences. The young man told him that he should come by anytime when he had fish or even if he did not have fish. Would he like a cup of coffee? He said he was Alberto Martinez from Colombia and living on the yacht for a while. He said that he was looking into buying some property nearby. Property that was right on the seafront. He told Peter that although he had grown up believing that Colombian coffee was the finest in the world, he had come to admire Jamaican agriculture and its products.

He was thinking of staying a long time and was very interested in meeting people in the town.

Particularly, people like Peter who knew the coastline and the waters very well, and about boats, and so on. The yacht had a sixteen foot tender with a fifty horsepower engine on it, and he would appreciate if Peter could take him out sometime exploring the reefs and coves.

He thought Peter was a very bright-looking youngster and he was keen on getting to know a few fellows just like him. Peter must stop by anytime whether he had fish to sell or not. He was quite sure that one day soon he could tell Peter about things that would interest him.

Mr. Martinez felt sure that Peter was a kid with ambition and, sooner or later, this business of catching a few dozen fish for a whole night's work would begin to get boring. But one could never be certain.

The Desperate Cycle

CHAPTER 20

THE DESPERATE CYCLE

Karen sat beneath the great window facing Mr. Akiyama from across the manager's wide mahogany desk. It was late afternoon and the sunlight was retreating upward from the valleys in a reverse replay of the morning version as it pulled the shadows back up the flanks of the mountains. The big clouds of the daytime heating skullcapped the peaks and cast their own special darkness in uneven purple patches.

"Yoshi," said Karen, "I want to ask you something."

"Is it about the transfer?"

"A bit about that, but not only that."

"It was bound to come eventually. I have been here many years, as you know. The letter was handwritten and signed by the president of our corporation himself. It was an expression of great courtesy and, observe, it was delivered to me by his personal assistant. That too is a measure of respect. I could hardly have expected more."

Karen shook her head. The ritualistic style of her employer's nation and company had always been slightly incomprehensible to her.

"There is no chance that I might go with you? Even to just see it? It looks so lovely in the pictures."

She had to say it. Like so many of those born on small islands, the desire to widen her horizons was a powerful driving force. It is estimated that half of all the Jamaicans in the world live outside of their native country.

Mr. Akiyama was a man who almost never said no directly to anyone. He looked at Karen with the gentle understanding which had always been his most powerful asset. It was not a contrived or false demeanor. It was the way he conducted his existence. He simply regarded it as correct behavior. Within reason, of course.

"When I get home I will institute the most detailed enquiries as to what I can do about that. There is nothing that would please me more than to be able to arrange for you to visit me. I am hoping that, in the meantime, you will do everything that you can to assist my young successor to conduct the new transition of expansion and all the other implementation of procedures that will come with laying out the two new adjoining farms. It is a most ambitious venture. It practically doubles our investment and at last affords us the opportunity to space the planting further back from the fence lines.

"I can quite understand why the home office might feel it would require the energy of a man half my age. And, you know, nothing will happen tomorrow. I have been given whatever time I feel is necessary to oversee the new arrangements. It may take up to a year. Again, that is the level of confidence they repose in me. The entire handover will be directed as I decide."

Karen considered that. A year was a long time. But she was not really a procrastinator by nature. "Yoshi, do you believe in God?" she asked.

Mr. Akiyama was a very well prepared man as a rule, but he had not quite expected that. Not from Karen. He had Rastafarian workers who frequently enquired if he knew that Haile Selassie was the one true living deity and that those who failed to recognize the conquering

Lion of the Tribe of Judah as the savior of mankind were destined to boil in black bubbling oil throughout eternity. To these devotees, he always replied politely that he was sure that this might well be so. But he never placed Karen in this category. He took a particularly close look at her face and wondered at what he saw there.

"It is a matter of personal privacy with me, Karen," he said. "But since you ask me directly, I will tell you what life and my scientific education has left with me. I see certain cycles in the history of this world which seem to have a driving force inherent within them. I do not know the name of this force, but it hardly seems to matter. It is there or it is not, and my belief in it will have no effect on it one way or another. It is not going to evaporate because I have the concept wrong.

"The one thing I feel reasonably certain about it is that it takes little account of any individual animal, plant, insect, fish or bird. It is immune to sympathy, recognition, or any other consequence other than one of which we poor tenants of a temporary residence must live in ignorance. So great is this cosmic force that the best we can do is try to carve out a tiny space of practical comfort and useful endeavor in the fleeting time frame within these great circles in which we enjoy existence. Anything beyond such an attempt appears to me to be arrogance.

"That is what I believe. But even the belief that I can understand that much may itself be arrogance. And arrogance is pride, and I agree with my Christian brothers that pride is probably the worst sin—if there is such a thing—that one can nurture. That is why it is a matter of personal privacy. I tell very few people. It is between us, my dear."

"You remember Joyce? The woman who married your friend, the Captain?"

"Of course I remember her."

"Well, she is my good friend, you know. She is a Christian now. Not a perfect one, she admits, but an earnest one. She figures that she will be a better Christian when she gets older and colder, as she says. She believes that a time of healing is coming. She says that all around her she sees signs of this. It is as though everywhere life is returning to happier times.

"She has a pastor friend who explains all this to her, day and night. He is a wonderful pastor in every way, according to Joyce, and he is certainly a fine-looking guy.

They spend a lot of time together. He explains things to her late into the night. He told her that the future is golden and that these cursed 'cycles' of misery, as you call them, and which really do seem to exist sometimes, are not real. He says God is coming to reclaim his world in joy and that is why happiness will return. The pastor says everywhere hope is returning.

"When she talks about it to me, I feel so good. Joycie says he makes her feel good, too. And then I saw the new plans for the coffee planting and how we are going to limit the trees to a boundary far back from the edges of the new plantations so that even when we use the insecticides, there will be a big area to absorb the residue. I understand that it will make it much more unlikely that it can run off down to the valley rivers. That's a sign, too. Don't you think it's a sign?"

Mr. Akiyama looked out over the now-dim landscape of the most beautiful mountain scenery he had ever known—more so even than the slopes of Mount Fuji which he revered dutifully as was patriotically appropriate—and tried to frame the sort of gentle measured reply he always was careful to make.

"It is possible I am wrong, Karen. Maybe a time of

perfection is coming. I do not really pray in the way that I suppose your friend Joyce and her pastor do, day and night, but I will try to pray that they are right. And pray that I have never done anything in my pride and my duty to make that impossible, although I have been faithful in my job and have had to make hard choices many times. I hope I am not part of some desperate, everlasting cycle. I particularly hope I am not a major contributor, but, like many other things, I am not sure about this either.

"I can tell you that I have long felt distress at the chemical agents that we must use and that's why I fought so hard for this expansion and the space for the new layout. It is something along the lines of that 'useful endeavor' I just mentioned. That I may not be here to see it completed is of no consequence. Nonetheless, I am pleased to have initiated it. I hope unforeseen events do not cause it to fail in some way. Now, since it is evening, come and sit with me near the window and watch the last of the daylight."

Sitting close by him, Karen knew with a conviction so powerful that it shook her soul and showed in her eyes that a time of perfection was coming—for her beloved island and its people.

A love of her country and hope for its future was so fierce that it ran like fire through her and made her feel as though she was suffering from a fever. So what if she never saw Japan, however pretty and orderly it must be? Her newfound faith glowed in her face and Mr. Akiyama, seeing this, felt an emotion that had been a stranger to him for almost the whole of his life. He felt the faint tugging of envy pulling at the carefully constructed cloak of satisfaction which he had woven around himself.

He thought of turning on the light, but decided he preferred to sit here with her as the fresh tropical night air filled the cool room, the temperature dropping almost by the minute. Mr. Akiyama appreciated the cold nights of the high mountains where he lived and worked. He was not, generally speaking, an admirer of heat.

CHAPTER 21

THE BREAKING STRAIN

> The prudent text-books give it
> In tables at the end—
> The stress that shears a rivet
> Or makes a tie-bar bend—
> What traffic wrecks macadam—
> What concrete should endure—
> But we, poor Sons of Adam,
> Have no such literature,
> *To warn us or make sure!*
>
> -Hymn of Breaking Strain (1935)
> by Rudyard Kipling

On some occasions, particularly in early summer when the weather pattern in the Caribbean is shifting from being under the winter influences of cold fronts, migrating southeast from the North American continent, to the summer domination of the waves of low pressure that cross the Atlantic from Africa, the classic "island weather" becomes unreliable. The most extreme example of this is, of course, a hurricane. But the more common occurrence is when these "tropical waves," as they are called, come over the land and produce lines of squalls and gusty conditions.

When one of these systems is in the vicinity of any of the islands, the classic shift to calm at evening followed by a cool breeze wafting from the mountains at night becomes distorted. The regular wind sequence may take a day or two to return to normal. These tropical waves are usually minor inconveniences only to people who have an intimate connection with such meteorological phenomena, such as farmers, captains landing aircraft, and members of the seagoing fraternity. They pass almost unnoticed by everyone else.

On a particular evening in the month of May, dealing with the residual effects of one of these minor disturbances in the climate, the recently qualified pilot on board the tanker, *Crystal Seas*, was working with only one tug. There were supposed to be two available to him, but the other one was engaged with a big container vessel at the other end of the harbor.

It was getting late and the shipping agent for the tanker asked the young pilot, "You don't think you can handle it or what? Ships have come alongside with one tug frequently. Regular procedure. Naturally, if that presents a serious problem to you, we can all sit here till morning. If that's what it takes to make you feel perfectly comfortable and stress free then, by all means, that's what we will have to do. We can certainly do that. We do not want to make you get all fretful.

"It is clearly recognized that you, Mr. Pilot, are the man to make this judgment call. We simply mention that we happen to have seen them dock regularly at this wharf with only one tug, and, in the old days, when we were already agents and you were not even born yet, they used to bring them to the wharf without any tug at all! Used to drop an anchor and work against that. But we wouldn't expect anything extraordinarily skillful and demanding like that from you. Just felt that we were not out of line commenting that it's getting late. It *is* getting late. That's all. But we fully understand that you, Mr. Pilot, are the man in charge. The young man in charge."

Now that a mention has been made of "the old days" and the connection between a heroic golden era from history and this venerable wharf has arisen, perhaps it might be instructive to glance back at the period when this particular structure was commissioned.

Back then, a thirty thousand ton tanker was a big one. Twenty or, perhaps, twenty-five was the normal size expected at this jetty. But the wharf was built to take a little more. After all, time does not stand still and we might get to forty thousand tons eventually. Such petroleum carriers might eventually have to come alongside here. What with that leeway, and the perennial shortage of funds to either maintain or replace anything in the Third World (whatever that means), the faithful, old platform had become used to today's seventy thousand plus ton ships leaning rudely on her frame and stood up to it, looking quite firm.

It did not feel quite so firm when a modern vessel rolled against it, but that was only for a brief moment. When that happened, you had to stand firm yourself if you were out on the end of the pier or you risked losing your balance when the surface moved underfoot as if in response to a submarine earthquake. Perhaps there were pilots that had never yet come to realize, being relatively young and in the period of invincibility through which we all must pass if we live long enough, how time works on all of us, wharves and men alike.

Foundations, especially those which rely on long uninspected pilings in salt water, weaken and become brittle. Maybe an X-ray can detect creeping deficiencies of this type in the bones of mankind and the iron skeletons of buildings, but Roentgen scans come under the heading of upkeep in general, and there's not a lot of that around here.

Times are hard. Budgetary constraints, like people not being able to afford medicine, come under the heading of *Facts of Life*. The public gets tired of hearing that kind of explanation all the time so it's generally better not to talk too much about such things. Boring and, more importantly, bad for the image of a proud independent nation. Rotten stuff for preserving morale borders dangerously close on being unpatriotic. Almost subversive.

The Danish-born captain of *Crystal Seas* spoke to the pilot from his position at the door of the bridge wing.

"Is the wind slackening a little? It really feels like it is. Shall we try to take her in, Pilot?"

"I think it is, too, Captain." The pilot picked up the VHF microphone. "Tug Port Antonio, take up the line. We're going alongside."

It's nine p.m. The wind off the ocean is still blowing, but is it a fraction less? Or just a variation of direction? Anyway, here goes. It definitely feels like a little lull. Maybe. And what do you think happens? There's a power cut on the wharf. Imagine that! Some worn-out circuit breaker, its guts eaten away by salt-induced corrosion, decides to quit, and suddenly, with the lights gone now, it becomes just a little more difficult to determine the exact distance separating the steel cliff-like side of the ship from the pier head.

The bright glare back on the land makes the distortion worse. You have all the illumination of the streets and houses behind the security lighting around the dock offices and then this sudden intervening pool of darkness. But in this moment of final approach to a mooring, it is very difficult to just stop and forget about it. Hardly practical, and so dreadful for the reputation of the man in command. *Can you handle it?*

The single tug has a line on the tanker and is pulling back, taking the way off her, slowing the forward momentum, but it still looks a little too fast. Just a little. There is only the one tug. So unfortunate! They have reverse power on the ship's main engine now, but it looks like perhaps it needs a little more.

"Do you think we could come astern harder, Captain?"

"Yes, Pilot." All the time, they are running out of wharf. God Almighty, is that the end of it just up ahead?

So they do what any reasonable man would do. They put more reverse on the main engine. What a pity a ship has no brakes! But ship handlers, like airplane pilots, have reverse thrust available. That's the only brakes they have. And it stops her, all right. She is roughly parallel to the dock now, with the long head of it ending where the left side of the ship turns inward to become the bow, but nothing to spare. Not an inch.

Now look at this awkward inescapable fact of physics—or is it hydraulics?—which escaped attention for just a few minutes while everyone was under such great pressure. This tanker has a left-hand pitched propeller, so when energy is applied to spin it in reverse, while increasing the stopping effect on the ship, it also causes the bow to swing slightly to port.

So a little of that solid seventy-thousand ton vessel is going to press pretty hard on one point of the good old veteran wharf. It will have engine power reinforcing the other pressure where the bulbous bow is going to contact the final piling holding up one end of the dock. And the damn, blasted, lovely, sea-scented, stinking, son of a bitching, southeast wind increasing the force applied. What happened to the lull? Hold your breath, boys. It should be all right. It has happened before and the man charged with putting a ship alongside has gotten away with it. Many times.

The old breaker was certainly within its rights to retire that night. It had every argument of neglect, age and decrepitude on its side. And now the structure, which depended upon the breaker for the electricity to provide lighting, decides that it will take advantage of the privacy of darkness to surrender to this assault on its fragile, generation-decayed, steel and concrete frame.

The whole end of the jetty collapses, but not totally. The heavy pipelines running back to the shore-side storage petroleum tanks stop it from joining the garbage and detritus which man and tractor and drains have pushed and poured onto the sea floor.

They were not built for that purpose, these pipelines, but they do what they can. They only crack a little. A flange opens as the ten bolts at the top of the arc snap off. The neatly sheared bolt heads rocket away into the night like shrapnel. Not a really big break, but enough. There's tons of it behind that opening. This is a delivery as well as a receiving wharf. And now even the strong wind can't hide that smell. Oil. Oil on water. Thick oil. Heavy, killing oil. Suffocating, blanketing oil.

The Desperate Cycle

CHAPTER 22

JAMAICA, NO PROBLEM!

In the daylight, there is less chance of hiding it. "What we have here," a distraught lady says, with frazzled hair—she had risen from her bed before daybreak when they called her with the news—and eyes like a startled, wounded bird, "is a harbor of oil."

That's the sort of exaggeration that brings these unhinged characters from the Environmental Trust into such well-deserved disrepute. Makes people laugh at them. There's plenty of water still sloshing around out there. There might be a bit of oil in it, but, really, "a harbor of oil?"

How does sensationalism assist at this juncture? What's wrong with these people? Do they have something against the government? Secret co-conspirators with the Opposition Party? Fancy saying something like that in a country famous for its tourist industry. Totally irresponsible. She looks like she needs a tranquilizer as well as a hair relaxer. Looks, and sounds, like she needs a complete relaxer. Perhaps a good crack on the top of her loony-haired head with a crowbar. Clearly a hysterical type.

A hasty press conference had been arranged. Officialdom must present the situation in a balanced way or leave crazy, lunatic presentations to undermine the balanced approach. A steady hand.

The Member of Parliament looked at his hand. The triple vodka and gin mix seemed to have steadied it nicely. It was rather early in the morning, but special occasions called for special measures. Chewing on a peppermint to avoid smelling of alcohol, he made his way to the podium. He assumed a steady gaze to match his hand.

"Now, let's get to the facts, ladies and gentlemen of the press," the Member of Parliament said in a super-steady voice without a trace of a slur. *Steadiness, steadiness,* he thought. "I know most of you, and you deal in facts. So I will give you the unvarnished facts. The facts are what counts. We are going to get booms and special detergents from abroad to deal with this problem. Let me rephrase that. We are going to get booms and detergents from abroad to deal with this *little* problem. Let's try to keep perspective here. That will take a tiny little while, but we are certainly going to get them. That's what we technical people call 'The Clean-Up Phase'.

"And, in the meantime, we don't fool around with even a very small oil leak. Even a very, very small one like we have here."

Jesus, I have to go easy here. I sound like a Monty Python skit.

"One of the pipes is already sealed off and the other one will be too, just as soon as we can get a new lock-off valve. It would have been controlled already, but the damn wheel on the old gate valve that should have cut off the supply to that—much smaller, by the way—pipe, came right off in the technician's hand along with the stem.

"A new one is on the way. Absolutely on the way as I speak. With a technical team from Galveston. That's a town in America where they know absolutely everything about oil. They had a river there that used to catch fire from surface spontaneous combustion and now it doesn't do it anymore. How do you like that? Pretty good, eh? When those boys get here, we will have the last minute, infinitesimal trickle stopped. As a minister in the administration, I have to keep on top of everything constantly. It's not easy, but that's what I always do.

"Good old nature is on our side too, as she so often appears to be. Just look at that wind! Keeping up really nicely, and all through the night. It had a lot to do with the minor accident, so the least it could do is help with the aftermath. A 'fair' wind, you could say. And that's exactly what it is doing. Helping. Breaking up the stuff on the surface water and some of the heavier material must be sinking, and the lighter components evaporating, or whatever, and the wind also helps with the smell in a most excellent way. Dispersion, they call it. Hardly a whiff!

"Thank you all, ladies and gentlemen. It is always great to talk with all you fine ladies and gentlemen of the media, and we will keep you constantly up to date and fully and completely informed. That's the way we do things, as you are all aware.

"If you know anything at all about me, you know I am a straight shooter. Transparency all the way. I look forward to seeing you all at the function at King's House tomorrow where I will be receiving my award for dedicated service to industry from the hands of our own beloved Governor General, representative of Her Majesty herself. Have a great day!"

Not bad, he thought. *At least nobody threw anything*.

The Desperate Cycle

CHAPTER 23

THE FINAL ROUND

From the marina, the watchman had heard the sounds of the impact during the night and knew something had gone dreadfully wrong across the harbor. It was just before dawn when he smelled the oil and knew what that meant.

Well, the watchman thought, *that's the end of it for a good long while. Me don't suppose me will live to see it begin to come back again. It was only barely showing the littlest signs it was coming back to life. Just last week the boy caught better than sixty pounds in one night. He got a Jewfish last week, and when last did anyone see one of those? Not a very big one, but a Jewfish for sure. And me did see two young pelicans flying over from where the old treatment plant is. Barton did tell me they were nesting again.*

In the early morning, after the disaster, he had seen the boy sitting on the stone breakwater looking at the dead eels. It takes a lot to kill those things. The boy was holding his head in his hands and his shoulders were unsteady. After a long time he got up and rowed his little oil-streaked skiff through the choppy, foul water and gone alongside Mr. Martinez's yacht. Even the sparkling Viking had a thick black coat of oil running along the waterline.

The boy had gone aboard, apparently at the invitation of Mr. Martinez. That was not surprising because the two seemed to have developed a rather unlikely friendship. The watchman hoped Mr. Martinez might be able to suggest something to the boy now that harbor fishing was surely destroyed. Perhaps Mr. Martinez could think of something. Something interesting.

Tony Tame

Consider this other fine book by Tony Tame:

The Village Curtain: A Jamaica Collection (2009)
by Tony Tame
257 pp. 5.25" x 8.5" Softcover
ISBN 978-0-9841175-0-5

A collection of fictional stories, sketches and imaginary characters set in the coastal communities of Jamaica. Meet a village elder who never questions his system of providing guidance, disillusioned providers of charity, sometime drug smugglers and a man who thinks the best way to harvest the ocean is to throw explosives into it.

Reviews of *The Village Curtain*:

"Characters in the book are treated with understanding.
The human spirit is strong."
                                    - Marie Gregory, *Caribbean Today*

"A collection of stories that are invariably about fishing,
fisher-folk and the sea, with vivid descriptions of the
geography and fauna of the locations...Refreshing."
                    - Paul H. Williams, *The Jamaican Daily Gleaner*

"A well written collection of fictional short stories
detailing the life struggles of the Jamaican fisherman."
                                    - Penny Cates,. *Goodreads*

The Desperate Cycle

ABOUT THE AUTHOR

Born in 1943, **Tony Tame** has been associated with the marine industry since the mid 1960's. After 1970 he became directly involved in the supply and service of equipment to the commercial fishing industry in Jamaica. His lifelong interest has been the methods used in various types of fishing and the people who work in this field. Still active in this field his fascination with these topics is undiminished.

The Desperate Cycle

If you enjoyed *The Desperate Cycle,* consider these other fine books
from Savant Books and Publications:

Essay, Essay, Essay by Yasuo Kobachi
Aloha from Coffee Island by Walter Miyanari
Footprints, Smiles and Little White Lies by Daniel S. Janik
The Illustrated Middle Earth by Daniel S. Janik
Last and Final Harvest by Daniel S. Janik
A Whale's Tale by Daniel S. Janik
Tropic of California by R. Page Kaufman
Tropic of California (the companion music CD) by R. Page Kaufman
The Village Curtain by Tony Tame
Dare to Love in Oz by William Maltese
The Interzone by Tatsuyuki Kobayashi
Today I Am a Man by Larry Rodness
The Bahrain Conspiracy by Bentley Gates
Called Home by Gloria Schumann
Kanaka Blues by Mike Farris
First Breath edited by Z. M. Oliver
Poor Rich by Jean Blasiar
The Jumper Chronicle - Quest for Merlin's Maps by W. C. Peever
William Maltese's Flicker by William Maltese
My Unborn Child by Orest Stocco
Last Song of the Whales by Four Arrows
Perilous Panacea by Ronald Klueh
Falling but Fulfilled by Zachary M. Oliver
Mythical Voyage by Robin Ymer
Hello, Norma Jean by Sue Dolleris
Richer by Jean Blasiar
Manifest Intent by Mike Farris
Charlie No Face by David B. Seaburn
Number One Bestseller by Brian Morley
My Two Wives and Three Husbands by S. Stanley Gordon
In Dire Straits by Jim Currie

Tony Tame

Wretched Land by Mila Komarnisky
Chan Kim by Ilan Herman
Who's Killing All the Lawyers? by A. G. Hayes
Ammon's Horn by G. Amati
Wavelengths edited by Zachary M. Oliver
Almost Paradise by Laurie Hanan
Communion by Jean Blasiar and Jonathan Marcantoni
The Oil Man by Leon Puissegur
Random Views of Asia from the Mid-Pacific by William E. Sharp
The Isla Vista Crucible by Reilly Ridgell
Blood Money by Scott Mastro
In the Himalayan Nights by Anoop Chandola
Rules of Privilege by Mik Farris*On My Behalf* by Helen Doan
Traveler's Rest by Jonathan Marcantoni
Keys in the River by Tendai Mwanaka
Chimney Bluffs by David B. Seaburn
The Loons by Sue Dolleris
Light Surfer by David Allan Williams
The Judas List by A. G. Hayes
Path of the Templar - Book Two of The Jumper Chronicles
by W.C. Peever

Soon to be Released:
Shutterbug by Buz Sawyers
Blessed are the Peacekeepers by Tom Donnelly and Mike Munger
The Lazarus Conspiracies by Richard Rose

http://www.savantbooksandpublications.com